The dog stood on the table, her head cocked

Fiona petted her clumsily, then picked up a fold of her skin. But she couldn't force herself to push the needle through.

"Like this," Jackson said. He moved behind her, crowding her into the metal of the exam table, and put his hands over hers. They were warm and a little rough, firm and gentle at the same time.

Familiar.

Yesterday, when he'd bandaged the cut on her arm, he'd been impersonal and quick. Businesslike. Nothing like the way he'd touched her years ago.

She'd been fooling herself if she thought she could forget what he felt like. Today his hands brought everything back in excruciating detail. The way he'd used any excuse to put them on her. The way he'd twined his fingers with hers. The way he'd touch her as if he couldn't get enough of her.

"Are you with me, Fiona?" he asked sharply, and she realized she'd been frozen, surrounded by Jackson, bombarded by memories.

"Yes," she said, shoving the images out of her head.

"Let's give it a try."

Dear Reader,

No matter what we achieve in our lives, there's always something in our past that makes us wonder what if? What if we'd moved to a different town? What if we'd chosen a different job or profession?

What if we hadn't broken up with our first love? What if we could go back and rewrite the story of our life? Is there anything we'd change?

Fiona McInnes wonders sometimes. She has what she wanted when she left Spruce Lake to study jewelry design—a thriving business and a career she loves. But she can't quite forget Jackson Grant, the man she left behind.

I loved giving Fiona, the third McInnes triplet, a do-over. And although I'm sad to leave Spruce Lake and the triplets behind, I hope you had as much fun reading about them as I had writing about them.

I love to hear from my readers! Visit my Web site at www.margaretwatson.com, or e-mail me at mwatson1004@hotmail.com.

Margaret Watson

HOME AT LAST
Margaret Watson

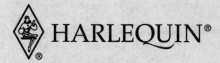

HARLEQUIN®

TORONTO • NEW YORK • LONDON
AMSTERDAM • PARIS • SYDNEY • HAMBURG
STOCKHOLM • ATHENS • TOKYO • MILAN • MADRID
PRAGUE • WARSAW • BUDAPEST • AUCKLAND

Recycling programs
for this product may
not exist in your area.

ISBN-13: 978-0-373-78299-4
ISBN-10: 0-373-78299-3

HOME AT LAST

www.eHarlequin.com

Printed in U.S.A.

ABOUT THE AUTHOR

Margaret Watson has always made up stories in her head. When she started actually writing them down, she realized she'd found exactly what she wanted to do with the rest of her life. Almost twenty years after staring at that first blank page, she's an award-winning, two-time RITA® Award finalist who has written more than twenty books for Silhouette and Harlequin Books. When she's not writing or spending time with her family, she practices veterinary medicine. She loves everything about her job, other than the "Hey, Dr. Watson, where's Sherlock?" jokes, which she's heard way too many times. She loves pets, but writing is her passion. And that's just elementary, my dear readers. Margaret lives near Chicago with her husband and three daughters and a menagerie of pets.

Books by Margaret Watson

For Nancy Good, my sister and my friend.

PROLOGUE

Twelve years ago

HER FATHER POUNDED violently on her bedroom door, and Fiona jerked. A drop of hot solder fell onto her hand, and the sudden, intense burn made her bite her lip to keep from crying out.

"What are you doing in there, Fiona?"

Sucking on her burned skin, she waited until she knew she could keep her voice steady. "I'm working, Dad."

The doorknob rattled. The latch she'd installed held tight. "How did you lock this door? Open it right now, or I'll take it off its hinges again."

Ignoring him, ignoring the throbbing blister already forming, Fiona turned off the soldering iron and carefully set it on its stand on her desk. She put the pieces of jewelry she'd been working on into her tackle box, then slipped the padlock onto the box and snapped it in place.

She drew back the bar latch she'd put on her door and opened it slowly. Her father stood there in his tweedy suit, glaring at her, his eyes cold and his mouth hard. "What have I told you about locking your—"

"Excuse me," she said, pushing him aside when he didn't move. "I need to use the bathroom."

Once inside, she collapsed onto the edge of the bathtub. She let cold water run over the raised blister on her hand until the pain subsided to a dull throb.

Maybe if she stayed in here long enough, he'd go away.

Even as the thought crossed her mind, she knew it was a foolish hope. Squaring her shoulders, taking a deep breath, she stepped into the hall.

Her father was gone.

Thank God.

She hurried into her room and stopped abruptly when she saw him on the floor, trying to open her tackle box.

"What are you doing?"

He stood up, brushing off his pants, smoothing back his carefully arranged hair.

"Why did you lock your door?" he asked. Her father had always believed that a good offense was the best defense. "What have I told you about that?"

"It's my room, Dad. I don't like you coming in without knocking. Without asking."

His expression darkened. "This is not *your* room. This is my house, Fiona. I can go wherever I want in *my* house."

She lifted her chin, tucking her hair behind one ear with a shaking hand. "You think it's all right to walk in on me while I'm getting dressed? Is that what you want?"

His face reddened. "Of course I don't. That's an ugly thing to say."

Fiona shrugged, her heart pounding, her palms sweating. "What am I supposed to think when you say you want to walk into my room whenever you feel like it?" She wiped her hands on her jeans. "It would make a nice story for that reporter who keeps calling about that stupid prize you won."

Enraged, he took a step toward her. "Stupid prize? You're calling the Pulitzer for fiction stupid?"

She was going to throw up. "Stop coming in my room. I'm seventeen. I have a right to some privacy."

"Privacy? So you can bring boys up here to do God knows what? Like that Grant kid who's been sniffing around you. He only wants one thing from you, you know. Once you give it to him, you won't see him again."

She'd already given Jackson everything she could, and he still loved her. "I've never had a boy in my room." The thought made her shudder. What she and Jackson had was magical. Beautiful. She wouldn't dirty it by bringing him into this house.

"Why aren't you downstairs?" he said, changing tactics. "It's almost time for dinner."

"I was busy. Working."

"On that amateurish junk of yours? You think someone is going to be interested in buying that?"

"Yes, Dad. I do." She *was* good. Her art teacher had told her so. Her friends all wanted her to make jewelry for them. Even her sisters liked it.

"Stop wasting your time, Fiona. You'll start college at Collier next year and find a real career. Maybe you'll become an English professor, like me."

"I hate English," she said. If he'd been a zoology professor, she'd have hated animals. "I'm getting out of this house as soon as I can."

"You're going to leave me alone?" His mouth twisted. "You're an ungrateful brat, just like your sisters. You'll be begging me to take you back in a month. Maybe less." He looked at the desk she'd made into a workbench. "You can't keep this junk in your room. That soldering iron is dangerous. I'm putting all of it in the garage tomorrow."

He stormed out into the hall, and she slammed the door behind him. Then she defiantly pushed the lock into place. "Fine!" she shouted. "I'll make a studio in the garage."

She waited for him to return, but he must not have heard her clearly, because he continued down the stairs.

Five hours later, after she heard her father snoring in his bedroom, she raised the blind and put a candle in her window. When a spray of tiny pebbles hit the porch roof beneath her, she blew out the candle, opened the window and climbed onto the roof.

Jackson was waiting when she reached the end of the trellis, and he caught her when she let go. Reaching up to throw her arms around his neck, she kissed him wildly. "You came."

"Of course I did. I saw the candle." He set her on the ground and took her hand. "I'll always be here when you need me."

She grabbed his T-shirt in both fists. "You think my jewelry is good, don't you?"

"Your jewelry is great," he said. "You're going to be a famous jewelry designer." He kissed her again. "You're going to put this town on the map. Everyone will know about Fiona McInnes in Spruce Lake, Wisconsin."

No! She wanted to be the famous Fiona McInnes in New York. The darkness hid the expression in his blue eyes and she tightened her grip on his shirt. Finally she let him go, smoothing out the worn fabric. They would work it out. She loved Jackson. He loved her. They'd be together forever.

"Let's go," she said, tugging on his hand. "I don't want to waste any time."

CHAPTER ONE

"THAT'S IMPOSSIBLE." Fiona jumped up from the desk in her father's home office and paced into the hall as she listened to the woman, one of the wholesalers who supplied her with silver and gemstones, on the other end of the phone. "There's been a mistake, Shelby."

"Maybe, but the check bounced. Sorry, Fiona. I can't send out this order until the bad check is cleared. I called Barb, but I couldn't get hold of her."

There was plenty of money in her business account to pay for the order of silver wire and lapis. Fiona took a deep breath. "Did you call Barb during the day?" Barb Lockley, Fiona's business manager, worked out of her apartment and she was meticulous about being available during business hours.

"Of course I did. I called several times but she didn't answer."

"There's been a mix-up somewhere,

Shelby," Fiona answered, her mind flying in ten directions. "Can I give you my personal credit card number until I straighten it out?"

"Sure." Shelby cleared her throat. "It'll have to be for both orders, though. When we get a bounced check, we need payment in advance for future orders."

"All right." It would put her perilously close to the limit of her credit card, but after she got hold of Barb, she'd go online and transfer the money to pay the bill. "Hold on a second while I get the card."

A few minutes later, Fiona tucked her credit card back in her wallet and paced the office as she punched in the number for her business manager. "Damn it!" This was what happened when you let personal stuff interfere with your business. She and her sisters had to finish dealing with this horrible house. And they needed to do it right away. She had to focus on her upcoming show. The Clybourne Gallery had a lot of influence in the art world.

The phone rang and Fiona settled on the edge of the desk. But she got a recorded statement that the number had been disconnected.

"What?" She stared at the phone, unable to believe what she'd heard. Maybe she'd pressed the wrong speed dial. Scrolling through her contacts, she dialed Barb's number. Same message.

Alarmed now, she phoned her agent. As she waited for him to answer, she sank into the old desk chair and accessed her business account on the computer. "David. Thank God. How come Barb's phone number is disconnected? What's going on?"

"I've been meaning to call you, Fiona," he said. "Barb seems to have disappeared. And your accountant called yesterday because she couldn't get hold of you. It looks as if Barb emptied the business account before she took off."

"What? Barb's gone? With my money?" She stood so quickly that the chair banged into the wall. "Why didn't you call me right away?"

"I've been trying to find her," he said impatiently. "I didn't see any reason to worry you until I figured out what was going on."

"No reason to worry me? This is *my* business, David. Have you forgotten that?"

"You haven't been acting like you cared about it," he shot back. "You've been out there in Hicksville for the past five months. I've begged you to come home and take care of your business, but you've always had an excuse."

"I have family obligations." She kicked her father's heavy walnut desk. "Apparently that means it's all right for you to forget I exist and my business manager to steal my money and disappear."

"I got you the gig at the Clybourne Gallery, didn't I?"

"I contacted Jules at the Clybourne," Fiona said.

"And I nailed it down. That's a huge step for your career, Fiona. But are you in New York, working on your pieces for the show? No. I haven't seen anything new from you since you've been in that godforsaken town." Fiona heard paper shuffling over the phone. "Sorry, babe, but with no new designs, your stuff has become stale. Orders are down. There's no buzz anymore."

"I'm working on pieces for the show," Fiona said, clutching the phone so tightly her hand hurt. "And when I talked about trying some different things, you said, and I quote, 'Don't worry, babe. Things are going great. Don't rock the boat.'"

"Guess I was wrong," David answered.

Fiona heard the faint clacking of a keyboard through the phone.

"Get off the computer," she said sharply.

"You're telling me my career is in the toilet and you're e-mailing someone else at the same time?"

"You're not my only client, Fiona," he said. "And some of them actually care about their careers."

His words terrified and enraged her. "Did you call the police about Barb?"

"Not yet. I keep telling myself there's an innocent explanation."

"David, the woman's phone is disconnected and there's no money in my business account." She'd wanted a well-known agent, someone with important clients in the art world. But she was a small fish in David's big pond. The realization tasted bitter in her mouth. "I thought you were on my side. But you're only on my side when the money is flowing your way. Once there's a problem, it's another story, isn't it?"

"Barb works for you," he said. "Not me. You should have been paying more attention to your career. Get your ass to New York, Fiona."

"I can't right now. I'm watching my nephew while my sister's on her honeymoon."

"Aren't you the little Suzy Homemaker?"

"David, I expect you to do something

about this. Call me by the end of the day, or you're fired." She snapped her phone shut.

As she stared at her bank statement showing that the balance in her business account was zero, she opened the phone again and called the police in Philadelphia, where Barb lived. "We'll put someone on it, ma'am," the bored-sounding officer said. "Give me your phone number, and we'll let you know if we find anything."

Translation—she wouldn't be hearing from the police anytime soon. "Thank you, Officer," she said.

Fiona stared out the window, numb. The impatiens she'd planted in the spring were in full bloom, a thick row of orange, pink and purple blossoms across the front of the house. The forsythia bushes she'd pruned were dense and bright green, clearly responding to her care. It was beautiful outside.

And her world was falling apart.

She swiveled away from the window and caught sight of the massive picture of her father leaning against the wall. They'd promised it to the college, but had stuck it in here, out of the way. He seemed to be watching her with that knowing sneer.

A very familiar sneer. The one he usually wore when he talked about her work.

"Why are you bothering with those little trinkets, Fiona? You're wasting your time."

"You'll never make a living designing jewelry."

"What are you doing out here? Playing with your silly beads again? Leaving me to cope with everything alone?"

"You're happy now, aren't you?" she said to the picture. "I bet you wish you were here so you could say *I told you so*. So you could tell me how stupid I've been, staying in Spruce Lake to take care of *your* business and neglecting my own. Oh, but wait. There was never any business more important than yours, was there?"

A hidden place inside Fiona burst open, and rage, pain and fear spilled out in a toxic tide. She picked up the Professor of the Year award sitting on her father's desk and hurled it at the painting. It tore through the canvas, obliterating the bottom of her father's head. But his eyes still stared at her.

"Damn you! You're dead and buried. Rotting in the ground. Get out of my life!" She grabbed one of his other Professor of the Year awards from the bureau and threw it at the picture, destroying the rest of her father's head. Then she smashed the third one repeatedly, until it broke into splinters of glass that went flying across the room.

"Professor of the year," she cried. "What did they know? You were a selfish, horrible man. We *hated* you. You should have died in that car crash. Not Mom. But we were stuck with you."

Fiona kicked the last box of her father's papers repeatedly, yellowing sheets cascading onto the floor. "You thought you were so important. I'm going to burn your precious papers."

She swept up an armful and stuffed them into the fireplace. Falling to her knees on the cold tile in front of the hearth, she grabbed handful after handful, stuffing them in until the only ones left were out of her reach.

A drop of moisture hit her hand, then another. Where was the water coming from? She looked down at her hands. She was crying.

She dug the heels of her hands into her eyes, trying to stop the tears. "I'm not crying for you, old man," she spat at the now-faceless picture. "I never cried when you died. You want to know what I did? I danced all night."

She staggered to her feet, looking for something else of her father's. Something she could destroy. Instead, she saw a man leaning against the doorway.

Even through the blur of her tears she recognized him. Jackson Grant. How long had he been standing there?

She froze, staring at his expressionless face for an agonizingly long moment. Then she stumbled backward, grabbing for the edge of the desk. "Jackson. Where did you come from? What are you doing here?"

"Hello, Fiona." His voice was as unreadable as his face. "Are you all right?"

"I'm fine." She knuckled away the last of her tears.

He looked at the torn picture against the wall. "You sure?"

"Yes, I'm sure." His hair was a darker blond and longer than she remembered. It curled above his collar, shaggy, as if he'd cut it himself. His shoulders were broad beneath the black T-shirt he wore, and his arms were ropy with muscle. Not the scrawny twenty-two-year-old she remembered.

Jackson had grown up.

And after she'd gone out of her way to avoid him in the five months she'd been in

Spruce Lake, he'd walked in on her at the worst possible moment. A witness to her humiliation. "What can I do for you?"

"Is that how you're going to play it? Pretending it didn't happen?" He nodded toward the papers in the fireplace, the broken glass on the floor, the ruined picture. "That was always your style."

"This isn't a good time for me, Jackson." He was the last person in the world she needed to see right now. She was shaky and drained. Empty. She wanted to curl up in a ball, bury her head behind her arms and block out everything about this house. This town. Her life.

"You're bleeding," he said, nodding at her arm.

A smear of blood covered her lower left arm, and a wide trickle slid sluggishly toward her wrist, where it dripped onto the floor. "I didn't see that." As she stared at it, her arm began to sting.

"Sit down." Jackson moved into the room and pushed her into the desk chair. "Stay there."

He jogged up the stairs. She heard him rummaging in the bathroom, and moments later he returned with bandages and gauze and a bottle of Betadine.

"Let me see."

She kept her arm close to her body. "I'll take care of it."

"Easier for someone else to." He dropped onto the desk and grabbed her hand. "I don't have time to play games," he said impatiently.

"What are you doing here?" she asked, trying not to notice the touch of his hands on her arm. And the memories they invoked.

He applied Betadine, leaving her arm stained yellow-brown, then examined the cut closely. An inch long and still seeping blood, it wasn't deep or dangerous.

Just stupid. Stupid to lose control like that, especially with an audience.

Even if she hadn't known she had one.

That's what happened when you lost control. You ended up embarrassing yourself.

As Jackson used gauze and the bandages to cover the wound, she struggled to repress memories evoked by the way his fingers felt on her skin. The way he smelled when he bent his head close to hers. The sound of his voice when he said her name.

Except now, his hands were impersonal and efficient. Just the way he'd be if he was taking care of one of his animal patients. "It doesn't need stitches," he said as he stood.

Putting distance between them. "Just keep it covered for a few days."

"Thank you." She resisted touching the bandage. "You didn't tell me why you're here," she managed to say in a level voice.

"I'm looking for my kids. They're supposed to be with Charlie, but I can't find them. This was the only other place I could think to look."

"Charlie told me he was hanging out at your clinic with Logan and Lindy." Saying their names hurt.

"They're obviously not there," he said, pacing the suddenly too-small room. "I called Charlie's cell phone, but he didn't answer."

It felt oddly intimate that Jackson knew her nephew's cell phone number. To realize Jackson was part of Charlie's life. Part of his inner circle. That there was a connection between them.

The way there used to be a connection between her and Jackson. It had been the elephant in the living room since she'd been in Spruce Lake. She drove Charlie to Jackson's clinic, picked him up there, ferried him to Jackson's house and back. All the while maintaining the fiction that she didn't know the town vet.

Unwilling to keep looking at him, she fumbled with her phone. "Let's try Charlie again."

That call went straight to voice mail. "He's either turned it off or the battery is dead," she said, standing. "He forgets to charge it sometimes."

"Where would he take them?" Jackson demanded.

"How do you know Charlie has taken them anywhere?" She bristled at the suggestion that Charlie was leading Jackson's kids astray. "Maybe *he* was following *your* kids."

"Not likely," Jackson said curtly. "He's older."

"By a few months!"

"He's smarter."

"My nephew is a great kid. He doesn't get other kids—"

"I'm not going to waste time arguing with you, Fiona. Logan and Lindy aren't where they're supposed to be, and I'm damned worried. Your nephew is with them. I would have thought you'd be worried, too." He headed for the door. "I'm going to look for them. Are you helping me or not?"

"Of course I am," she said, grabbing her purse. "Maybe they went for a run. Charlie has been talking about doing cross-country at school this fall." She glanced at Jackson out of the corner of her eye. "Logan and Lindy are the ones who got him interested in it."

"For God's sake, Fiona," he exploded. "This isn't a pissing contest. They're *all* missing. I'll drive south of town. You go north. Here's my cell phone number."

He looked around for a pen and paper, and Fiona grabbed one of the sheets left on the floor. She ripped off two pieces, gave him her phone number and watched him write his. Then she hurried out the door without waiting for Jackson.

Thank goodness none of the Spruce Lake cops were around as she sped out of town. She was a mile or so into the countryside when she saw two kids ahead of her. Logan and Lindy. They were crouched over a third kid.

Charlie. She bit her lip, holding back a cry. He was lying on the shoulder of the road.

CHAPTER TWO

NOT BOTHERING TO PULL OVER, Fiona threw the car into Park and leaped out, leaving the door open as she raced to the kids. "Charlie! What's wrong?" she called, her heart racing. He'd been hit by a car while he was out running a couple of months earlier. *Please, God, it hadn't happened again.*

Charlie jumped up, brushing bits of gravel off his shirt and shorts. "You scared it away, Aunt Fee. What's the matter with you, yelling like that?"

Fiona skidded to a stop. "You're okay? You're not hurt?"

"Of course I'm not hurt," he said scornfully.

"Then why were you lying on the ground?"

"We were looking at a fox snake." He pushed up his glasses and gestured toward the side of the road. "They're really cool snakes because they rattle their tails in the grass when they're startled. I was showing

Logan and Lindy." He scowled. "Until you came along."

"You were messing with a rattlesnake?" Her voice rose, and she struggled to remain calm. What would Jackson think when he found out her nephew was poking at a rattlesnake in front of his kids? "What were you thinking?"

"It was a fox snake." He enunciated each word, as if she were a slow child. "Not a rattlesnake. Fox snakes brush their tails through the grass to mimic rattlesnakes. Jeez. Don't you think I know the difference?" A boy and a girl stood behind Charlie, staring at her.

"I have no idea, Charlie," Fiona said sharply, relief giving way to anger. "You said it was *rattling* its *tail.*"

"What are you doing here, anyway?" he asked. Smart kid. He knew when to change the subject.

"Dr. Grant is looking for Logan and Lindy. He came by the house because he thought you all might be there."

"Uh-oh," Logan said under his breath.

Charlie kicked at the gravel on the shoulder of the road. "We wanted to go running, and he was with a client."

"You didn't think to leave him a note? Or

tell the receptionist?" She took a deep breath and turned to the Grant kids. Logan looked just like Jackson—the same dark blond hair, the same eyes and mouth. Lindy was tall and thin with light brown hair and an angular face that would be striking in a few years. She must take after her mother.

Fiona tried to give the two kids a friendly smile. "Hi, I'm Charlie's aunt Fiona."

"I know who you are," Lindy said. "My dad bought me some earrings when you were in that store in town."

"Oh, right, the Pieces show." Fiona winced. She hadn't been at the show. She'd wanted to stay in New York and she'd persuaded her sister Zoe to take her place. Of the triplets, Fiona and Zoe were the identical ones. "Are you enjoying them?"

"I love them." She touched her ears. "I don't wear them when I run. I'm afraid I might lose them."

"I have some clear plastic backs you can put on the hooks to keep them from falling out. I'll make sure you get a pair."

"Yeah?" Lindy's eyes widened. "Cool."

"Let me call your father and tell him I've found you." She punched in his number. "Hey, Jackson, I've got them. They're on

County U. They went running. I'll bring them home."

"No. I've seen you drive. I'll be right there."

"Listen, buddy, I'm not the one who had two accidents—" Too late. He'd hung up. "Jerk," she muttered.

Lindy's smile faded. Was she worried that her father would be mad? "Are you okay?" Fiona asked the girl.

"How do you know my father?" Lindy demanded.

"What do you mean?" Fiona asked cautiously.

"You sounded like you know him really well," she said, sticking her chin out.

Whoa. What was that about? "Your father and I grew up together in Spruce Lake," Fiona explained. "I've known him forever." She tried to smile.

"He doesn't want a girlfriend," Lindy said. "So don't get your hopes up."

"Lind, knock it off." Logan's face was bright red.

"I'm not his girlfriend," Fiona said.

"But you want to be, don't you? I can tell."

Fiona shaded her eyes from the sun. "Does your father know how rude you are to strangers?"

"It's not rude when it's the truth. I can tell what you're thinking. I heard the way you talked to him."

"Lindy, knock it off," Charlie said, kicking the gravel on the side of the road. "Aunt Fee doesn't want to be your dad's girlfriend. That's gross."

Lindy turned on Charlie. "Lots of women come into the clinic to see my dad, but their dogs and cats aren't really sick. They ask him for his cell phone number." She glared at Fiona. "He doesn't need a girlfriend. He has me and Logan."

"Cut it out, Lindy," Logan said, grabbing his sister's arm. She jerked away from him. "You're embarrassing me," he said in a low voice. "Charlie, too."

Lindy shoved him, and he stumbled into the tall weeds. "You want him to get a girl-friend, Logan? You know what will happen."

If only the girl knew how hard Fiona had tried to avoid Jackson. "Lindy, you have nothing to worry about. Your father and I are just two people who knew each other a long time ago."

They'd been so much more than that. They'd been each other's entire universe.

Until Fiona dumped Jackson to go to New York. But that was none of Lindy's business.

"Yeah, right."

Fiona's patience dissipated. "You know what, Lindy? Think what you want. I don't really care."

The girl stood with her hands on her hips. "You can leave now," she said. "My dad knows where we are."

"Forget it, you little brat," Fiona said. "I'm not leaving until Jackson gets here."

Logan tried to pull Lindy away, and the twins scuffled until they heard the roar of a truck. Moments later, Jackson's pickup appeared.

JACKSON'S HEART finally slowed when he rounded the curve and saw his kids standing on the shoulder of the road. "Thank God."

He pulled up behind Fiona's car. She'd left her door open. A car going in the other direction would take it right off. He pushed it closed as he walked past.

"Logan. Lindy." He stopped in front of them and took a deep breath, trying to control his immediate reaction. After suffering through their mother's frightening eruptions, the last thing they needed was their father screaming at them. "What are you doing out here?"

"We wanted to go for a run," Logan said. "We didn't want to bother you."

Jackson counted to five. "What have I told you guys?" he said, hoping he sounded calm and rational. "You have to let me know where you are and what you're doing."

He glanced at Fiona, who was standing to the side, her arms crossed over her chest. Fresh blood stained the bandage. "You're bleeding again," he said to her.

She glanced down at her arm as if she'd forgotten all about the cut. "I'll change the bandage when I get home."

"Let me see it." When she didn't extend her arm immediately, he stepped in for a closer look. It's just seepage," he concluded. "You'll be fine."

"Thank God. I was thinking amputation," she said as she tried to pull away from him.

His hand tightened on her momentarily, then he let her go. "Smart-ass," he murmured.

Her snarky little cracks used to make him laugh. He'd always loved her mouthiness. And the way she'd tormented him.

Lindy edged closer. "Why did she come looking for us?"

Oh, God, here we go again. "Two of us

could cover more ground, and Ms. McInnes was worried about Charlie."

"She was yelling at us."

"I was not," Fiona said. She frowned at Lindy, clearly annoyed.

Why did Lindy have to pull this with Fiona? "Lindy, haven't we talked about this?"

His daughter shrugged one shoulder. "Tell her she can leave," Lindy commanded. "I told her earlier, but she wouldn't go."

"Lindy, apologize to Ms. McInnes. Right now."

Lindy glared at him, then at Fiona.

"Lindy," he warned.

"Sorry," she finally said.

"Now get in the truck. We'll discuss this later."

As she ran toward the truck, Lindy looked over her shoulder and stuck her tongue out at Fiona's back. "Lindy!" he yelled.

She scurried into the truck and slammed the door.

He turned to Logan. "You and I have some talking to do, too."

"We're not babies, Dad. Can't we even go for a run by ourselves?"

Why did both of his kids have to pick today for major attitude? "You know the rules,

Logan. You have to let me know where you are. Since you didn't, and I had to come looking for you, several clients and their sick animals had to wait to see me."

"Sorry," he said, his expression hunted. Jackson had no trouble interpreting it. His boy didn't want to be corrected in front of his friend's aunt.

"Get in the truck," he growled. Logan hurried away.

"I'll wait in the car, Aunt Fee." Charlie edged away from him and Fiona.

So Jackson wasn't the only one who called her Fee. Memories unspooled in his head as he turned to Fiona.

"Thank you for helping me look for them," he said.

"You're welcome."

He'd pushed Fiona and the scene in her father's office out of his head. He hadn't been able to focus on anything besides his kids. But now that he knew they were safe, he remembered her obvious devastation. "Are you okay?" he asked. "You were pretty upset back at the house." He'd been shocked at the anger spilling out of her. Anger directed at her father.

Anger he understood too well. He'd hated

John Henry McInnes with an intensity that had been almost frightening. He'd blamed her old man for driving a wedge between him and Fiona.

"I'm fine," she said coolly. "Sorry Charlie led your kids astray."

She made it sound as if Logan and Lindy were innocent, and he knew that wasn't the case. "I'm sure Charlie wasn't completely to blame," he admitted. "I'm just glad we found them so fast."

"Me, too," she said. "So long, Jackson."

She turned and headed toward her car, and he couldn't help watching her go. The long, lean body he'd loved was a little curvier now, a little fuller. Fiona was a woman, not a teenager. Her hair was short and spiky, the ends dyed bright pink. But she still loved to wear cutoff overalls. The sides gaped, giving him a shadowed glimpse of one breast, covered by a yellow T-shirt.

She stopped at the old Honda Civic and said something to Charlie, who was leaning against it. Then she turned to face him.

"You shut my car door."

"Yeah. Another car could have taken it right off."

She sighed. "My keys were in the ignition,

and now the door is locked. With the engine running." She kicked the tire. "Damn it."

"Do you have another set of keys?"

"At home."

He nodded at his truck. "Hop in. I'll take you to get them."

"There's no room," she said.

"There's a jump seat. You and Charlie can fit there."

Fiona glanced at the cab of the truck and bit her lip. "Why don't you take Charlie to get them? I'll wait here."

Evidently, she didn't want to be in there with Lindy. "It's ninety degrees out here, Fiona. There's no shade. It'll take five minutes."

"But…" She closed her mouth. "Fine. Thank you."

He opened the door and waited while first Charlie, then Fiona climbed into the jump seat. Her overalls tightened across her rear end and he looked away.

"What's going on?" Lindy demanded as he swung into the driver's seat.

"I locked Ms. McInnes's keys in her car. We have to take her and Charlie home to get her extra set."

"That was pretty stupid, Dad," Lindy said.

"Lindy! If you're smart, you'll keep your

mouth shut." Jackson glanced in the rearview mirror and caught Fiona's eye. She gave a tiny shake of her head.

Maybe she understood. Fiona had had a difficult parent, too. But sometimes he wanted to kill Mallory for what she'd done to their children.

They all rode in silence until they reached Fiona's. "Thanks, Jackson," she said as she and Charlie scrambled out of the truck. "I appreciate the ride."

"How do you plan on getting back to your car?" he called after her.

"Not your problem," she said over her shoulder. "I know you have clients waiting."

He jumped out of the truck and slammed the door. In a few long strides he'd caught up with Fiona. "Get the damn keys. My clients can wait five more minutes." He hesitated. "Lindy had a hard time when her mother left."

Fiona's expression softened. "Yeah, I got that, Jackson." She glanced at the truck. "Okay. I'll be right back."

She disappeared into the old brick house and the front garden caught his eye. A thick row of purple and pink flowers bracketed the front steps. More flowers were massed behind them. He'd bet it was Fiona's work—after her mother died, she'd always done the gardening.

She appeared in the doorway, a key and a black fob clutched in her hand. "Got them," she said as she ran down the steps. Being careful not to brush against him.

"Great." He sneaked a peek at his watch. Clients would be backed up in his waiting room. "Let's go."

Lindy was slumped in the front seat, her arms crossed. Logan straightened as Jackson got closer. Clearly, he'd been talking to his sister. They both looked angry.

"You two okay?" he asked cautiously.

"Lindy's a loser," Logan said.

"You're a jerk-face," his daughter shot back.

"Stop it, both of you." He opened the door for Fiona. "Lindy, get in the back so Ms. McInnes doesn't have to squeeze in."

"It's okay," Fiona said. "I'm fine back here."

Lindy glanced over her shoulder, triumphant.

Fiona met his eyes in the mirror, and he saw only pity in them. For Lindy? For him?

He didn't want pity from Fiona.

He had no idea what he *did* want, but it sure as hell wasn't that.

CHAPTER THREE

"THIS IS NOT just a missing person, Officer," Fiona said firmly. "Barb Lockley stole money from me before she disappeared."

"I'll transfer you to one of the detectives," the man responded wearily.

"Thank you," Fiona said. "I'd appreciate that." She heard a click as she was put on hold with the 40th Police District station in Philadelphia. Just then the doorbell rang.

Holding the cell phone to her ear, she walked to the front. Through the screen, she saw a delivery man in the familiar brown uniform. "Great," she said, opening the door. "You have my equipment."

"Nope." The young man gestured toward something at his feet. "I have your dog."

"What dog? I don't have a dog."

A white plastic crate sat on her dad's porch. Behind the wire, a small tan dog rested its head on its front paws, its resignation suggesting it couldn't believe the mistake, either.

The delivery man wiped his forehead with his forearm and shoved an electronic tablet at her. "The dog's been on the truck for an hour and it's hot back there. You'll want to get him inside. Sign at the X, ma'am."

"That's not my dog. You're supposed to be delivering a package of dental picks and pliers." Fiona's hand tightened on the phone she still held to her ear.

The delivery man scrolled up on the tablet. "You Fiona McInnes?"

"Yes."

"Is this eight-one-six Parkwood, Spruce Lake, Wisconsin?"

"Yes, it is. But…"

"Then this is your dog." He held out the device again. "Just sign it, ma'am. I have a lot more deliveries." He nodded at the carrier. "Looks like a letter on the crate."

Fiona glanced at it. Scrawled across the envelope in familiar bold letters was her name. Her stomach tightened into a fist. "Meredith. What the hell did you do?" She looked at the dog again and her memory stirred. "Annabelle?"

The dog's tail thumped once.

"I don't know anything about this," Fiona said as the dog got to its feet.

"Not my problem." He waited, and Fiona finally took the tablet and signed her name.

Without another glance, the delivery man ran down the front porch steps, jumped into his truck and sped away.

Still holding the phone to her ear, Fiona carried the crate into the house and pulled out the letter. As she read it, she sank onto the stairs.

"I'm going to kill her," she said as she tossed the paper to the floor.

"What did you say?" A male voice in her ear spoke sharply. "Where are you? Who are you going to kill?"

Fiona closed her eyes. Of course the police would choose that moment to pick up. "It was a figure of speech, Officer. I got a package from a friend."

"Where are you located?" the man persisted.

"I'm in Wisconsin. There's no one here but me and the dog my best friend just dumped on me. Since I haven't mastered the art of killing someone with evil thoughts, you have nothing to worry about."

"Where in Wisconsin are you?"

"Spruce Lake," she said. "Eight-one-six

Parkwood. All right? Now can we get back to why I called you?"

"Hold on a minute."

Fiona could hear him writing it all down.

"Okay, why did you call us?"

Ten minutes later, frustrated and angry, Fiona closed her phone. The detective would have one of the patrol officers check Barb's house. They'd call her when they had any information.

The dog sat in its crate, staring at her. It hadn't moved during her conversation with the police. "What am I supposed to do with you?" Fiona asked it.

The dog thumped its tail once. Fiona tried calling Meredith. "Your mom ran off to Brazil with her new lover," she told the dog as she listened to the phone ring. "She says he's 'the one.' That's why she dumped you on me. She says she knows I'd want to adopt you. Like hell," she muttered.

When she got Meredith's voice mail, she said, "Call me. Right now. What the hell is wrong with you? I'll be back in New York in three weeks and I can't keep a dog at my condo. You know that. So what am I supposed to do with Annabelle? What were you thinking?" She snapped the phone shut.

Annabelle cocked one ear but didn't stir. Fiona knelt and studied the dog. "What are we going to do about this?" she asked. She opened the crate, but the dog lay there and watched Fiona with big brown eyes.

"Annabelle?" Fiona said uneasily. She didn't know anything about dogs, but shouldn't it want to get out?

Finally, Fiona reached inside and pulled. The dog was wet. Fiona scrunched her nose at the pungent smell of urine. "Oh, Annabelle," she said. "No wonder you didn't want to come out."

She carried the dog into the laundry room and put it in the sink, where Annabelle flopped to her belly again. Fiona ran upstairs and grabbed a bottle of shampoo. When she returned, Annabelle was where she'd left her.

Before she could turn on the water, the front doorbell rang again. "Hold on a minute," she called. "Stay there, Annabelle," she said. The dog didn't raise her head.

When she got to the door, she found Police Officer Jamie Evans waiting for her. "Hey, Jamie. How are you?"

"A little pissed off right now. We just got a phone call from the Philadelphia police about a possible homicide at this address."

"You've got to be kidding me."

"Do I look like I'm kidding?" Jamie scowled. "Damn it, Fiona, what's going on?"

She opened the door. "Come on in. I'll show you."

Jamie trailed her to the laundry room, where Annabelle lay in the tub. "That's what's wrong," she said.

"A dog? You threatened to kill a dog?"

"No, I threatened to kill my best friend who sent me this dog, and the police overheard me." She explained what had happened, and Jamie's lips twitched.

"Good one, Fiona. You never did know how to keep your mouth shut."

"Get out of here, Jamie. I have a dog to wash."

"If that friend of yours shows up in Spruce Lake, call me before you do anything rash," he said as he walked out.

Fiona rolled her eyes, then returned to Annabelle. During her bath, the dog lapped at the water coming out of the faucet. As Fiona toweled her off, she studied the dog.

Tan hair stood up in clumps all over a skinny body. A lot skinnier than the last time she'd seen Annabelle. The dog's ribs and spine were sharply outlined beneath thin skin. And her skin looked rough and dry.

Holding on to the dog, Fiona found a bowl and filled it with water. Annabelle showed the first signs of life as she strained to get at it. As soon as Fiona put her on the floor, Annabelle began lapping up the water.

She didn't stop until it was empty. Fiona filled it again and watched as Annabelle drank half of it.

Charlie clattered down the stairs, calling, "Aunt Fee?"

"In here," Fiona answered, and listened as her nephew opened the refrigerator.

A few moments later he appeared, eating an apple. He paused when he saw the dog. "What the heck is that?"

"This is Annabelle." She tried to smooth the dog's hair so it lay flat.

"Is it supposed to be a dog?" Charlie asked. "Because it looks like a rat. A rat with a hairy tail."

"According to the letter that came with her, she's a Yorkiepoo."

Charlie hooted. "Sounds like something you'd step in on the sidewalk."

Fiona watched in concern as Annabelle lay still. "She hasn't really moved since she got here."

Charlie dropped to the floor and held out

his hand. The dog staggered to her feet and wobbled toward him, sniffing at his apple. She licked it, and Charlie grinned. "She likes apples."

"There's something wrong with her," Fiona said. The dog was trembling on spindly legs as she tried to eat Charlie's fruit.

"She's probably hungry. I'll get her a piece of the chicken from last night," Charlie said.

When he returned with the meat, Annabelle gobbled it down, then vomited.

"She's sick."

"Let's take her to Dr. Grant," Charlie said. "He'll know what's wrong."

She wasn't going anywhere near Jackson after what had happened earlier in the day. The memory of him walking in on her tantrum still made her face burn. "Not Jackson. Is there another vet in Spruce Lake?"

"Why would you want to go to another vet?" Charlie asked. "Dr. Grant is awesome. And you know him already."

"That's true, but he's probably really busy," she said, grasping at straws. "He said his clients were backed up while he looked for you and his twins."

"That's stupid," Charlie said, as only a

twelve-year-old could. "You have to find out what's wrong." Then his expression brightened. "Are you afraid of blood? I'm not. I'll take her if there's going to be blood."

"I'm not afraid of blood." As tempting as it sounded, she wasn't going to take the coward's way out and send Charlie to Jackson with the dog, who was now lying on her side. "He can't be the only vet in town."

"He is," Charlie assured her.

"All right," she said, looking at the dog. "I guess we have to take her to him."

Fifteen minutes later they pulled up to the small white building that looked more like a house than a veterinary clinic, with its black shutters and row of bushes out front. Fiona held the towel-wrapped dog carefully and walked inside.

A cheerful young woman said, "Hi. Welcome to Spruce Lake Veterinary Clinic." Then she saw Charlie. "Hey, Charlie. Is this your dog?"

"Nope. My aunt just got her."

Fiona waited while the woman filled out some papers, then she and Charlie followed her to a small exam room. Jars of cotton balls and tongue depressors sat on the counter next to the sink, along with a box of tissues, a liquid soap dispenser and a thermometer. The small space was immaculate.

"It'll be a few minutes," the young woman said. "He got a little behind his schedule."

Her fault. And Charlie's. Fiona cringed inwardly.

Charlie shifted from one foot to the other, clearly excited, but dread twisted Fiona's stomach into a knot. She *so* didn't want to be here. She squirmed every time she remembered looking up to see him standing in her dad's doorway.

Below Charlie's soothing conversation with Annabelle, Fiona heard the rasp of paper against plastic, the slide of a folder from the basket on the door. She waited for the door to open, but the silence from the hall stretched unbearably long. Her heart beat against her chest and she held the dog more tightly.

Finally the door opened and Jackson stepped in, dressed in blue surgical scrubs. He studied Annabelle for a long moment, then looked up. Impossible-to-read blue eyes met hers. "Hello again, Fiona. Busy day for you." He smiled at Charlie. "I didn't know you had a dog."

"It's Aunt Fee's," Charlie said. "We think it's sick."

"Let's take a look." Without looking at her,

Jackson reached for the blanket-wrapped dog, his fingers brushing Fiona's arm. He set Annabelle on the table and unwrapped her.

Fiona moved out of his reach. *Damn it.*

Apparently unaware of her, Jackson ran his hands lightly over the dog's back, his fingers spanning her ribs and moving down the bumps of her spine. Fiona couldn't tear her gaze away from his long fingers. Years ago, his hands had been soft and caressing one moment, clever and urgent the next.

Now they were thorough and gentle as he examined Annabelle. He brushed the clumps of hair apart and checked her skin. He looked in her mouth and her ears, listened to her heart, felt her abdomen. Then he turned to Charlie. "Logan and Lindy are in the kennel, giving Maxine a bath," he said. "You want to hang out with them for a while?"

"Sure!" Charlie practically bounced on his toes as he dashed out of the exam room, clearly familiar with the clinic.

When the door closed behind him, Jackson finally looked at her. This time it was easy to read his expression—barely controlled anger. "I suppose you just noticed her condition this morning," he said. She opened her mouth to answer, but he didn't give her a chance to speak. "Oh, wait, you've been busy, haven't you? Don't bother, I've heard all the excuses in the book. What the hell is wrong with you, Fiona? Why do you even have a pet?" His hands hovered over Annabelle, as if he was protecting the dog. "I guess your jewelry is still more important than anything else."

"For your information, Jackson, she's not—"

"Save it," he interrupted her. "It's been a long day and I don't have time to listen to excuses."

"Fine." Did he really think she'd neglect an animal? That she would let her dog get to this point and not notice? "What's wrong with her?"

"For starters, she's badly dehydrated. Does she have water available all the time?"

"She drank a bowl and a half right before we came over here," Fiona answered, biting off the words.

"She's eating a lot, isn't she?" he asked.

"She was trying to eat Charlie's apple. I thought that was kind of strange. Then she scarfed down some chicken and vomited."

"I think she has diabetes. I'll have to do some blood work and check her urine, but I can smell the ketones on her breath. You'll have to leave her here."

Diabetes? Not only had Meredith dumped Annabelle on her, but the dog was sick. How was she supposed to deal with a diabetic dog along with everything else that was going on? "Is that as serious as it sounds?"

"No point in talking about it until we know if that's what's wrong with her." He ran his hands over the dog, and Annabelle leaned into him. "Why is she wet?"

"I had to give her a bath. She…had an accident."

"That's been happening a lot, I'll bet."

Her temper flared and she finally snapped. "Listen, you arrogant ass. For your information, that isn't—"

"Aunt Fee?" Charlie appeared in the door, his hair soaking wet and plastered to his head. "Is it okay if I stay here awhile? I need to help the twins."

Fiona took a deep breath and forced a smile. "Who's getting the bath, Charlie? You or the dog?"

Her nephew grinned. "Maxine's pretty feisty."

"Then I guess you'll have to give them a hand. What time should I pick you up?"

"I'll bring him home after we close," Jackson said.

"All right. Thank you." Calmer now, she waited until Charlie disappeared and said, "I'll call tomorrow to see how she's doing."

Jackson assumed she would neglect a dog. He thought she was an uncaring woman who wouldn't notice or care if her pet was sick.

A man who held that opinion about her didn't deserve her time, or the effort it would take to correct him. She had nothing to say to Jackson.

"I'll have the results of the blood test after ten."

"Fine." She brushed past Jackson as she reached for the door. He smelled of disinfectant and soap and animals. But beneath the odors of his clinic, potent. Sexy. Male.

Damn it.

Somehow she made it into her car. This was twice in one day that Jackson had her at a disadvantage. That he'd seen her at her worst.

Or thought he had.

Her chest hurt as she drove home, and she told herself it had been a tough day.

It had nothing to do with Jackson.

FIONA SLID a frozen meal into the microwave and watched it spin. Charlie was eating with the Grants.

She'd welcomed the idea of being alone. To work on her jewelry. To have time to settle herself.

But instead of enjoying the quiet, she was all too aware that this had always been her father's house. She missed Charlie and all the activity and commotion a preteen brought with him. She missed her sisters. They'd been in and out since she'd arrived back in town five months ago.

But Bree was on her honeymoon with Parker, and Zoe and Gideon were still self-absorbed newlyweds. Just like when they'd been kids, she was the last one living in the house. Tonight she was alone, and there was nothing to keep the ghosts at bay.

She hated this damn house. At night, in particular, the ghosts spoke to her. The ghost of her mother, protecting her girls from their father's rages. The ghost of her father, asking her why that Grant boy was hanging around. The ghost of Jackson, waiting by the window as she snuck out of the house at night to meet him.

Her memories of Jackson were inextricably bound with this house. He'd been her escape, her refuge. He'd been her lover. They'd been each other's first, and they had learned together. And even though they'd started out clumsy and awkward, they'd fit together perfectly.

For Fiona, more perfectly than any lover since.

The front door opened as she was eating her microwaved lasagne. "Hey, Aunt Fee. I'm home," Charlie called.

Fiona tossed the tasteless food into the trash.

She forced herself to smile as she stepped into the hall, then stopped abruptly. Jackson stood near the door. Charlie had already disappeared up the stairs.

"Jackson." He wore an old blue polo shirt that reminded her of one he'd had in high school. His jeans were faded and molded his thighs like only well-worn jeans could, and his hair was ruffled from the wind. "What are you doing here?"

He shoved a hand through his hair, making it even more disheveled. "I owe you an apology."

"For what?" she asked. She folded her arms across her chest and leaned against the wall, prepared to watch him squirm. She wasn't going to make it easy for him.

"Why didn't you tell me she wasn't your dog?"

She shrugged. "You were too ready to

believe I'd neglected her." She'd rather die than let Jackson know how much his immediate, careless assumption had hurt.

He sighed. "I pride myself in not jumping to conclusions. I didn't give you a chance to explain. I'm sorry."

"No big deal." She pushed away from the wall. "It's not like I care about your opinion of me."

His jaw tightened. "You made that perfectly clear a long time ago."

"I'm not in the mood for reminiscing," she said. "Tell me about Annabelle."

He studied her for a moment, and now she was the one squirming. He used to be able to see through her as if she were made of glass. She hoped her defenses were better now.

He gave her a tiny nod. "Annabelle it is. She does have diabetes."

"How did she get it?"

"It's not uncommon in older dogs. Especially females. No one knows exactly why."

"Can you fix her?" She thought about Annabelle, lying in her own urine in that crate, and her throat tightened.

"We can treat her. We can't cure her."

"So what do I have to do?"

"Nothing, right now. I've started her on

fluids and insulin. She'll have to stay in the clinic for a couple of days."

"What about after that?"

"There's a lot involved in treating a diabetic dog." He raised his eyebrows. "You'll be seeing a lot of me for a while."

CHAPTER FOUR

THE ODOR of pine disinfectant enveloped Fiona as she stepped inside Jackson's clinic. The clean smell should have been nothing out of the ordinary at a vet clinic. But the pine reminded her of her youth. Of Jackson.

He'd cleaned his house several times a week with that pine cleaner, after one of his father's binges. She'd smelled it on his hands too many times to count. When she inhaled deeply, she was back in the past.

She might as well admit that the past wasn't going away. That it had meant something.

Jackson had meant something. He'd been more important to her than anyone else in Spruce Lake besides her family.

There was no reason they needed to be enemies now. No reason to fight. He'd apologized last night for jumping to conclusions. He'd be treating Annabelle. They had to work together.

They could get along. They were both adults who'd matured past the roiling emotions of adolescence. Now they could be friendly acquaintances.

Pleased with her mature decision, she eased the door closed and walked up to the desk. Lindy Grant was sitting in the desk chair, bent over a sketchbook, a pencil in her hand. She was clearly lost in her own world.

A pair of lapis earrings dangled from her ears, the tiny gold flecks in the blue stones reflecting light from the overhead fixture. FeeMac earrings? As the girl worked, she absently reached up and rubbed one between her fingers.

Fiona softened as she watched the girl. Lindy had been rude and unpleasant, but she was a twelve-year-old girl with raging hormones and mood swings. A girl who'd been abandoned by her mother.

Fiona knew how it felt to be twelve and suddenly motherless. You desperately needed stability and security, and anything that threatened that stability was frightening.

Lindy looked up at that moment and saw Fiona watching her. She cupped a hand protectively around her sketches, then slammed the book closed.

So much for empathy and connections.

JACKSON HAD HEARD the small click of the front door opening, followed by footsteps in the reception area. Then nothing. He tossed his pen onto the desk. Damn it, Lindy was supposed to have locked the door fifteen minutes ago. Now, in spite of the stack of records to be written up, he'd have to see whichever client had wandered in late.

Maybe it was just someone who needed to pick up medication or food.

"Hello, Lindy." It was Fiona. "I came to see my dog, Annabelle."

"We're closed," Lindy said. "You'll have to come back tomorrow."

Oh, God. Here comes a train wreck. Jackson finished scribbling on the chart he was writing up.

"All right," Fiona said. "I like your earrings. Are they FeeMac?"

"Don't you recognize your own stuff?" Jackson heard the scowl in his daughter's voice. "You helped me pick them out. I guess you don't remember."

"Oh, of course," Fiona said. "Right. Are you enjoying them?"

Damn it. He knew that tone of Fiona's voice. Defensive. Protecting secrets. And he knew exactly why Fiona hadn't remembered selling Lindy the earrings. He stood and shrugged into his lab coat.

"They're okay," Lindy said.

They're okay? Lindy adored the earrings. She wore them almost every day.

"I brought those plastic earring guards I told you about. I was going to give them to your father, but now I can give them to you instead."

He reached the end of the hall in time to see Fiona pull a small plastic bag from her purse and hold it out to Lindy. His daughter hesitated for a long moment, then accepted it. "Thanks," she said grudgingly.

"You're welcome." Fiona smiled. "I'm having another show at Pieces soon, if you're interested."

Lindy dropped the plastic bag on the counter. "FeeMac jewelry is stupid."

Fiona reared back as if Lindy had slapped her. "I guess I won't be seeing you, then."

"You wouldn't remember me anyway. You didn't last time."

"Oh, I'll remember you, Lindy," Fiona said.

"That's enough, Lindy," Jackson said,

stepping into the room. "Please lock the front door. Hello, Fiona."

Fiona nudged the tiny plastic bag on the counter. Then she squared her shoulders and looked at him. "I'm sorry, Jackson. I came to visit Annabelle, but I didn't realize you were closed. I'll come back tomorrow."

"As long as you're here, you might as well see her."

She hesitated, glanced at the door. Deciding whether to bolt. It had always been easy to read her. She took a deep breath. "Thank you. I'm worried about her."

"She's back here." He turned and walked toward the surgery area door, aware of Fiona behind him. Irritated because all he could smell was her citrusy scent, even over the strong odors of animal and disinfectant.

As soon as the door closed behind her, Jackson said, "I apologize for Lindy. Again. She's…we're…" He sighed. "I'm sorry. She's had a rough time."

Fiona nodded, but she was guarded. Closed off. "I won't take it personally."

That would be damn hard when Lindy meant it personally. "I'll talk to her again."

"Don't worry about it." She gave him a dismissive smile that made him want to put his hands on her, just to see if he could rattle her. "I'm not going to be seeing much of Lindy, am I?"

"She spends a lot of time here in the summer."

"Then I'll have to make sure Annabelle stays healthy."

"She was right about one thing, though." He leaned closer. Just to gauge her reaction. "You and Zoe were up to your old tricks again, weren't you?"

"What do you mean?" she asked warily.

"At that store in town. Where you were supposed to be helping the customers pick out jewelry. That was Zoe."

"Busted." She exhaled and shrugged. "I couldn't get away from New York, so I talked Zoe into covering for me."

"I thought there was something off that day." He'd walked into the store and felt nothing when he saw her. He thought it meant he'd finally been cured of Fiona McInnes.

Then he'd walked into her dad's house and had a relapse.

"My daughter thinks she has jewelry picked out for her by the famous Fiona McInnes," he said, lowering his voice so Lindy couldn't hear.

"Clearly she's not too impressed about it."

He remembered Lindy's remark about

Fiona's jewelry being stupid. "She didn't mean that. She wears those earrings all the time."

"I'm guessing she won't be wearing them much anymore." Her voice was cool, but she bit her lip. He remembered the small, telltale sign that she was anxious about something.

Why was she anxious? Not because a kid made a snarky remark about her jewelry. Fiona was tougher than that.

Not his business, he reminded himself. Nothing about Fiona was his business. Except for her dog.

"Oh, she'll wear the earrings," Jackson said. "Too many of her friends are jealous because you picked them out for her. Except you didn't, did you?"

"I probably would have chosen the same thing," she answered. "The lapis suits her."

"That's not the point," he said, trying to rattle her. Damn it, why was he worrying about her anxiety? Not his business. Hadn't been for a long time. "The point is, you lied to all those customers. Including my daughter."

She watched him, her eyes as blue as Spruce Lake. Eyes now as chilly as the water in winter. "I'll give her another pair of earrings, Jackson. Then she'll have a pair that I picked out. Now where's my dog?"

She'd retreated into that shell where no

one and nothing could reach her. And he didn't care anymore about breaking it down. "In here," he said, struggling to regain his professionalism. "She's better today."

He stopped in front of Annabelle's cage and the dog stood up, wagging her tail. Another dog barked and two cats rubbed against their own cage. "You're feeling better, aren't you?" he murmured to the dog as he opened the door. "You want to come out?"

Annabelle sniffed his hand, and Jackson picked her up.

"She looks so different."

Fiona's surprise irritated him. He set the dog on a table in front of the cages. Had she thought he was going to neglect Annabelle? Or mistreat her, because he had a grudge against her owner? "Of course she looks different. She feels better."

Fiona slowly approached and held out her hand. Annabelle licked her fingers, and Fiona began to thaw. She petted the dog gingerly.

"She's due to eat again in a few minutes," he said. "Stay here with her and I'll get her dinner."

He measured out some canned food and put it in a cardboard feeding bowl, then set it on the table. Annabelle practically inhaled it.

"When can she come home?" Fiona asked.

"Tomorrow at the earliest. Maybe the next day. You have to be ready to take care of her."

"I know how to take care of a dog." She touched Annabelle's head.

"Not a dog with diabetes," he retorted. "Do you know how to give an injection?"

"What?"

"You're going to have to give her insulin shots every day. Can you do that?"

She stared at him, then looked at the dog. "I have to give her a shot? Every day?"

The Fiona he remembered could do anything she set her mind to. "I'll teach you how," he said. "If you can't give her a shot, you can't take her home."

"I won't leave her here."

"You'd have to find someone else to take care of her. Or put her down."

"Put her down?" She recoiled, then drew the dog closer. "That's cold, Jackson." She looked at him as if he'd suddenly grown a second head.

He was cold? Fiona was the original ice queen. She'd walked out on him without looking back, even after he'd begged her to stay. Tamping down his frustration, he said, "If she doesn't get insulin, she'll get sicker and sicker until she dies. And it won't be an easy death."

Before Fiona could answer, Lindy opened the door and slipped into the room. "Is that your dog, Ms. McInnes?"

"She is now. This is Annabelle."

"She's pretty ugly, isn't she?" Lindy said.

"She's sick," Fiona answered, smoothing the dog's light brown hair. "She's very pretty when she's well."

"We have big dogs," Lindy said, as if big dogs were the only ones worth having. "They're golden retrievers."

Jackson listened, wondering what had gotten into his daughter. The kid who'd begged him for a small dog. A dog that could sit in her lap.

"Yeah?" Fiona said. "What are their names?"

"Maxine and Kinky."

"Kinky? That's an unusual name." She glanced at him, then quickly away. She stood stiffly against the table.

Was Fiona not as immune to him as she'd like him to think?

Did he care?

"Kinky ran around in circles a lot when he was a puppy and got his leash tangled," his daughter said, unbending a little. "I'm the one who named him."

"It's a great name," Fiona said.

Lindy shrugged one shoulder. Jackson had no trouble reading the tension in the air. "Get your stuff together, Lind," Jackson said. "We have to pick up Logan."

Her eyes narrowed. "It is together. I'm ready to go." She stood there, looking from him to Fiona.

"Go wait in the office," he said, more sharply than he intended. "I have to talk to Ms. McInnes about her dog."

She hesitated for a moment, then walked out, dragging her feet. And she left the door open.

Jackson reached over and pushed it shut. "What happened the other day between you and Lindy? She's had a few problems lately, but nothing on this scale. She's acting as if she hates you. What did you say to her?"

"Why are you assuming I said anything to her?" Fiona lifted her chin.

"Are you telling me that a twelve-year-old kid picked a fight with you?"

"Do you think I'd say or do something to hurt your daughter?" she asked. She held the dog so tightly Annabelle yelped. "Do you think I'm that cruel?"

"I don't know, Fiona. After you walked

out, I came to the conclusion that I didn't know much about you at all."

"Here's something you can take to the bank. I'm not going to say much to either of your kids. To be honest, I don't want anything to do with them. I'd rather avoid them completely."

"What the hell is that supposed to mean?" he said, bristling. "What's wrong with my kids?"

"Nothing's wrong with them." She set the dog carefully on the table and ran her hand down its back. "I'm sure they're great kids. It's what they represent."

"I don't have any idea what you're talking about, Fiona," he said, watching her stroke the dog. Annabelle arched her back into Fiona's hand.

The way he'd craved her touch a long time ago.

"I know how old they are, Jackson. I know when they were born."

"What does that have to do with anything?" he asked. What was she talking about?

"I hadn't even been gone a month when you got their mother pregnant. I felt guilty for a long time because of the way I left. Clearly, I was a fool." Her throat rippled as she swallowed. "Were you sleeping with both of us?"

He stepped backward, his mouth open. "What the hell kind of question is that?"

"If I had gotten pregnant a couple of weeks after we broke up, wouldn't you be asking the same thing?"

He drove his hand through his hair. How was he supposed to explain what had happened with Mallory? "You don't understand."

"You're right. I don't. But I'm not asking for an explanation. I don't care anymore."

"Are you blaming *me* for the way we broke up?" he said, stunned when her words sunk in.

"I'm saying that since you got another woman pregnant right after I left, maybe what went wrong with us wasn't completely my fault. Every time I see your kids, I'm reminded what a fool I was to think so." She slung her purse over her shoulder. "I'll come by tomorrow so you can teach me how to give Annabelle her shots. What time?"

She wasn't going to walk out with the last word. "Right now," he said. "Right now is a good time."

"You said you were closed. You have to pick up Logan." Her hands tightened on the dog.

"Stop stalling, Fiona," he said. "You're going to have to do this. And now is the perfect time to learn."

CHAPTER FIVE

THE STARK WHITE walls and cold metal of the equipment closed in on her. She wasn't ready for this, Fiona thought frantically. She hadn't had time to psych herself up to give Annabelle shots.

Which was exactly why Jackson wanted to do it now. Payback for her remarks about his twins and his ex-wife.

Fiona glared at him. Nodded once. "Fine. Let's do it now."

"Stay here with her while I get what we'll need," he said, watching her warily. Was he expecting her to collapse because she had to give her dog a shot?

Annabelle looked up at her with those trusting brown eyes, and Fiona's hand faltered as she petted the dog. "It's for your own good," she whispered. "To make you feel better."

The dog didn't understand, thank God.

Because Fiona felt like a complete hypocrite. All Annabelle would know was that Fiona was sticking a needle into her.

Was it like this when you had kids? When they had to get a shot and you told them it was for their own good? Did they feel lied to and betrayed?

Jackson walked back into the room with a handful of thin syringes, a small bottle of what looked like water and a thick plastic bag, half-filled with a clear liquid. "Okay, we're set." He absently smoothed his hand over Annabelle. "Are you ready?"

Fiona wiped her hands down the sides of her overalls. "Of course."

Jackson set the dog on the floor, then he picked up one of the syringes and showed her how to draw liquid from the bottle. He explained the numbers on the barrel of the syringe, then he handed it to her. "Okay, you're going to inject that into the top of this IV fluid bag. It's thick plastic so it will feel a little like you're going through Annabelle's skin."

Jackson sounded objective and professional. As if it was no longer personal for him. That was good. Because she couldn't concentrate on both Jackson and Annabelle.

She took the bag, but it felt awkward, like

trying to hold Jell-O. As she bobbled it, Jackson steadied it from the bottom.

"Hold the bag at the top," he said, demonstrating. "Then you're going to push the needle through one side. Don't go through both sides." His hands brushed hers, his touch businesslike and efficient. Impersonal.

The same way he would interact with any client.

She was thinking about his hands as she touched the needle to the bag. It was tougher than she expected, and she pushed harder. The needle passed through both sides, and water from the syringe squirted across the room.

She felt like an idiot.

"Not quite so hard," Jackson said. He nodded at the wall. "I'm going to paint a bull's-eye there, considering the number of people who hit it on their first try."

Was he trying to reassure her? To make her feel better? Or was he laughing at her?

She couldn't tell.

It didn't matter.

She was going to do this if it killed her.

She grabbed the bottle and drew another dose.

This time, she managed to push through only the first layer of plastic and injected the liquid into the bag. After repeating it a few more times, Jackson picked the dog up off the floor and set her on the table.

"Now try it on Annabelle."

The dog rasped her tongue over Fiona's hand, and Fiona dropped the syringe. How was she supposed to give the damn dog a shot when she licked her fingers?

"It's got to be routine. You have to be able to pop the shot into her without a second thought," Jackson said. "Don't think. Just do it."

"You've been doing this for years," she said. "You've had plenty of time to think." But she picked up a fold of Annabelle's skin between her shoulders and got ready to inject. Then Annabelle looked over her shoulder at her.

Her hands shook and when she pushed the needle through Annabelle's skin, it came out on the other side. The dog yipped and the liquid dribbled onto her hair.

Fiona dropped the syringe. "Oh, God. I hurt her."

"No, you didn't." He handed her another one. "Try again."

Annabelle stood on the table, her head cocked. Fiona petted her clumsily, then picked up a fold of her skin again. But she couldn't force herself to push the needle through.

"Like this," Jackson said. He moved behind her, crowding her into the metal exam table, and put his hands over hers. They were warm and a little rough, firm and gentle at the same time.

Familiar.

She'd been fooling herself if she thought she could forget what he felt like. Today, his hands brought everything back in excruciating detail. The way he'd used any excuse to put them on her. The way he'd twined his fingers with hers.

The way he'd touched her as if he couldn't get enough of her.

She remembered the feel of his body against hers, as well. Too clearly.

"Are you with me, Fiona?" he asked impatiently.

"Yes," she said, shoving the memories out of her head.

"Let's give it a try." Molding his hands to hers, he pushed the needle into Annabelle's skin, and she felt the little pop as it went through. Jackson's fingers lingered a second longer, then they dropped away. She wanted to protest, to tell him she needed help again.

The stress must be affecting her brain.

He had her repeat the process two more

times, by herself. Finally he asked, "Can you do that by yourself? At home?"

"I don't have a choice, do I?"

"No. But you can practice some more before you leave. I want to be sure you're comfortable with this."

Nothing about this was comfortable. "I'm afraid I'm going to hurt her." She touched the dog lightly on the head, and Annabelle lifted her nose.

"She doesn't feel much," he said. "Just a tiny pinch. She'll handle the injections fine."

The unspoken *better than you* hung in the air.

"You're enjoying this, aren't you, Jackson?"

"Enjoying what?"

"Seeing me rattled like this. Having trouble giving the dog her shots."

"Of course not," he said. "I want you to learn how to do this. You'll need to give Annabelle shots twice a day."

"And it had to be right now."

He shrugged. "You were here. I had a few minutes. Seemed like a good idea."

"Really? And here I thought it was retaliation because I brought up your ex-wife and wondered whether you were banging her at the same time you were doing me."

Emotion flickered in his eyes. "Not at all.

Although I don't think we were finished discussing that."

"Of course we are." She gave him the cool, screw-you smile she'd perfected to deal with suppliers and distributors. "Your personal life is none of my business."

"You brought up the past." His eyes skimmed over her, and it felt as if he'd touched her. "I guess you're not so over me, after all, Fee."

Her heart lurched at his use of her nickname. "Don't flatter yourself, Jackson. I got over you a long time ago. When I heard about your twins."

She scooped up Annabelle and walked out the door.

"HEY, AUNT FEE! Look who I got to bring home!" Charlie stood in the door of her studio, a long-haired black cat draped over his shoulder.

"What the heck is that, Charlie?" she said, dropping the pliers and dental pick she'd been using and putting the intricate piece she'd been working on in a foam-encased box.

"It's Tasha." He grinned. "I wasn't supposed to get him until Mom and Parker got back from their honeymoon, but there isn't room for him in the clinic anymore, so Dr. Grant said I needed to take him today."

"Jackson gave you a cat?" She struggled to keep her voice steady. She knew what he was up to. He hadn't liked that she'd had the last word yesterday.

She was going to kill him.

"It's okay," Charlie said, setting the cat on the concrete floor. "Mom knows about Tasha."

Fiona stared at the animal. She'd never seen a cat that size. "Are you sure that's a cat? If she was any bigger, you could put a saddle on her and go for a ride."

"Yeah," Charlie said happily, bending down to pet the cat, who arched into his hand. "Isn't he great?"

"He? Tasha is a male?"

"Yeah, Lindy named him," Charlie said, rolling his eyes. "I told her it was a stupid name." He pulled a paper bag out of his backpack. "Dr. Grant said to give you this. He said you'll need it for Annabelle."

There were two prefilled syringes in the bag, and a note. *Insulin for the mutt. You need to come in and get a supply.*

The veterinary receptionist she'd spoken to that morning had promised to send a supply home with Charlie.

Fiona had expected a lot more than two doses.

Tail in the air, Tasha strolled the studio, sniffing everything. He stared at Annabelle, asleep on a pillow at Fiona's feet. Then, before Fiona could stop him, he leaped onto her table and plopped down on the amethysts she'd been using.

"Hey, Tasha likes your jewelry, Aunt Fee," Charlie crowed.

She snatched the box holding her project out of the way. "Get him off my table, Charlie McInnes. Right now."

"Okay." Charlie plucked the cat from the table. As he swung him toward the floor, Fiona saw something glittering in his fur.

"Wait a minute. He's taking my stones with him." She hurried around the table and patted the cat down, finding three of the purple gems. "Charlie, check him again."

As Charlie ran his fingers through the cat's fur, Tasha fell onto his side, purring loudly. In spite of her irritation, Fiona smiled. "Looks as though Tasha likes you, kid."

"Yeah, we're buddies." He slung the cat over his shoulder again. "He's clean. No diamonds. I'll get him out of here."

"You're taking him to your father's house, right?" Fiona asked.

"Can't do that," Charlie said. He fiddled with the cat's collar. "Melody is allergic to cats."

So she had to deal with a sick dog and the world's largest cat while she was trying to track down her business manager and find her missing money. At the same time she was getting ready for her make-or-break show at the Clybourne Gallery. "And the reason you didn't wait until your mom got home was…?"

"Dr. Grant has a bunch of animals coming in to board this weekend and he needed Tasha's cage. You'll hardly know he's here," Charlie assured her. "I'm taking care of him. That was the deal I made with Mom."

"Dr. Grant didn't have one empty cage?"

"Nope," Charlie said. "That's what he told me."

"Just keep him out of my studio."

She fumed as Charlie closed the door and headed for the house. Not one empty cage in the whole clinic.

My ass.

She reached for her cell phone, then hesitated. If Jackson was trying to irritate her, she was just playing into his hands. Better not to say anything.

She was patient. She could wait.

Jackson would find out that payback was a bitch.

CHAPTER SIX

"THANKS FOR CLEANING cages for me, Charlie," Jackson said wearily as he turned onto Parkwood late in the afternoon. "I'll make sure you get paid."

"You don't have to pay me, Dr. Grant," Charlie said. "It was fun." The kid squirmed. "Besides, my Aunt Fee would kill me if you did."

"Is that so?"

"She told me before you picked me up that I couldn't take any money. She said that helping you out today was the least I could do after I've hung around your house and eaten your pizza all summer."

"That doesn't matter. You work for me, you get paid." He glanced at the boy. "You did a nice job," he said quietly. "You were organized, you kept Logan and Lindy focused, and you got the work done. If you'd like a part-time job when you're older, let me know."

"Yeah? How about right now? My mom would let me."

"You're a little young to work, Charlie. You're supposed to be having fun during the summer." The kid didn't know that childhood disappeared way too fast.

"Working at the clinic *is* fun," he said eagerly. "And I'm trying to save money to get an emerald tree boa."

"A tree boa? Those are nasty snakes," Jackson said as he pulled to the curb in front of the McInnes house. "I had to treat one in vet school. No matter how often I handled him, he struck at me every time. I hated that little snot by the time it went home."

"Really?" Charlie shoved his dark hair from his eyes. "I hadn't heard that. I'll have to do more research, I guess."

"Yeah, check those bad boys out before you plunk down your money." He nudged the boy with his elbow. "Thanks again, Charlie."

As Charlie climbed out of the car, Jackson spotted Fiona sprawled on her back on the front lawn. She was resting on her elbows, her face tilted to catch the sun. Her breasts strained against the faded denim of her cutoff overalls.

She'd always liked wearing overalls. Without a bra.

He let his gaze linger on the swell of her chest. The sight transported him back to a night at Spruce Lake, years ago. Light from the moon and the stars shimmered on the water. He could see Fiona stand and walk out of the lake as if it was yesterday. Water sluiced down her body like a waterfall of diamonds. The moonlight made her skin glow like pearls. His blood heated at the memory of the way she looked, the way she'd felt in his arms when she nibbled on his ear and asked him to warm her.

Breaking the spell, Charlie trotted over and crouched next to Fiona. She sat up and the denim sagged away from her chest.

Just as well. He'd been thinking about Fiona too much lately. He didn't need to have the image of her and her soft curves stuck in his mind.

She spotted him and paused. She said something to Charlie, then stood and sauntered over to the car.

Fiona's walk was burned into his brain. If he couldn't see her face, smell her scent or hear her voice, he'd recognize her by the way she moved. Loose limbed, self-confident, unconcerned about anyone's opinion of her.

He rolled down the window as she approached the car. "Hello, Fiona."

"Jackson. Thank you for bringing Charlie home."

"It's the least I could do. He did me a huge favor by cleaning cages today. My kennel kid didn't show up." Again. He'd have to light a fire under Michael's butt. The joys of owning a small business.

"I could have picked Charlie up."

He nodded toward where she'd been lying in the grass. "It would have been a shame to disturb your busy day."

"Good one, Jackson. I was going to turn into one of those white-skinned, blind creatures that live in caves if I didn't get some sun. I've been in my old studio since six this morning, working." She rested her forearms on the open window. "And taking care of that so-called cat you gave Charlie yesterday."

"You don't like Tasha? He's a great cat." He only felt a pang of mild guilt for sending the cat to her. He really had needed the cage.

"I'm sure he is. He snuck into my studio this morning. By the time I got rid of him, he'd spilled two containers of beads on the floor. It took me most of the morning to find all of them."

He eyed her carefully. Why wasn't she mad? Fiona had a fierce temper.

"You shouldn't have let him in," he said, figuring that would set her off. He didn't want to examine why he was baiting her.

She lifted one eyebrow. "I'll make sure and explain that to him next time."

"I thought you were coming to the clinic today. To pick up the rest of the insulin and syringes you'll need."

She slapped the edge of the car. "I completely forgot. Go ahead and charge me for the missed appointment. I'll come in tomorrow."

"We don't charge people for missed appointments," he said. "That's a big-city thing."

"And you're just a small-town good old boy, aren't you, Jackson?" She smiled seductively.

He couldn't tear his gaze away. He'd seen that mouth in his dreams for years. He'd woken in a sweat countless times to reach for her…even when he'd been married. Mallory had deserved better than that. Even after he would realize where he was, who was next to him, he couldn't forget the taste of Fiona's lips, the touch of her tongue, the nip of her teeth.

She leaned against the door, close enough that her unique fragrance washed over him. Close enough to touch.

"Fiona," he began, then he stopped. What

was he going to say? That he dreamed about her? Still wanted her?

He'd given her his heart once and she'd thrown it back at him. Then she'd walked away without looking back.

He rested his arm on the steering wheel. "I'm going to regret this, but I have to ask. Why aren't you pissed off at me about Tasha?"

"Who says I'm not pissed off?"

"Then why aren't you yelling at me?"

She smiled. "I've learned a few things since I left Spruce Lake. Revenge *is* a dish best served cold."

"Now I'm scared."

"Just out of curiosity, Jackson, why did Charlie have to bring the cat home yesterday? As opposed to a couple of weeks from now when Bree's back."

"I wasn't trying to irritate you, Fiona." That had just been a nice side benefit. "I needed the cage, that's all. This is the week before the college starts to gear up for the fall semester, and everyone from the professors to the janitors takes a vacation. They all want to board their pets with me, and I have a waiting list as long as my arm. It happens every year."

"Is that right?"

A shadowed suggestion of cleavage at the front of her gaping overalls, partially hidden by her V-neck T-shirt, distracted him. He was almost certain she wasn't wearing a bra. "Uh, call the clinic and talk to Debbie. My receptionist. She'll tell you the same thing. We call this hell week." He shook his head. "Probably why my kennel kid didn't come in today."

"I'll take your word for it." She stood, hiding the view. "I'd better go make Charlie's dinner before he cleans out the refrigerator. See you tomorrow. When should I come in?"

"Sometime in the morning. I'll have the insulin and syringes ready by then."

"Right."

He didn't pull away until she'd disappeared inside the house. It was just polite to wait and make sure she got in safely.

His reluctance to leave had nothing to do with the sight of Fiona's hips swaying as she walked.

"YOU ARE POSSESSED," Fiona said to Tasha as the cat lounged on the floor in her studio the next afternoon. "You know that, don't you?"

The cat had been hiding behind the flowers in the backyard. He'd darted into the studio when she'd opened the door, eluding her easily when Fiona tried to grab him. And while Fiona erected a barrier around the edge of her table to keep the cat from jumping onto her work space, Tasha had watched her intently.

Probably calculating the weak spot in her defenses.

When Tasha stretched a rear leg in the air and languidly cleaned the inside of his thigh, Fiona smiled in spite of herself. "Think you're pretty hot stuff, don't you? Just remember I can toss you out of here anytime I want."

With a final glance at the cat, who was now sitting Sphinx-like on the floor, Fiona pulled out one of her sketchbooks. She'd filled it with new ideas a few months ago, then reluctantly put it away when her agent and her business manager urged her to continue with the same old, same old.

Apparently the same old, same old wasn't working anymore. It was time she took control of her own career.

Her heart beat a little faster as she looked through the sketchbook. These designs were edgier than typical FeeMac jewelry, more angular instead of rounded, the emphasis on the metal more than the stones.

Some of them were meant to be done in

gold rather than silver. Up until now, silver had been her signature metal.

The designs were risky all the way around.

Perfect for the show at the Clybourne. She needed to take some risks to revive her career.

She swiveled her chair and opened the safe she kept behind her table. She had plenty of silver, but no gold. Gold was expensive, and she couldn't afford to buy more than a few ounces right now.

Until the police found Barb and got her money back.

Fiona removed two spools of silver wire, then closed the safe. If she couldn't afford gold, she'd start with silver. But she was going to start something. The show was in less than a month, and her old designs weren't going to cut it. She needed something new.

She had no idea how much time had passed when someone began pounding on the door. She jerked and bumped the table, scattering the pieces of silver she'd painstakingly cut into specific sizes. "Come in, damn it."

Jackson walked in. "I figured you were in here."

"Where else would I be?" Her heart thudded. He used to sneak into her studio when her father was at the college.

She rarely got much work done while he was there.

"Oh, I don't know. At the clinic, maybe? Picking up that insulin and those syringes?" He scratched Annabelle's head. She'd trotted over as soon as he opened the door.

Fiona looked at her watch, shocked when she saw what time it was. "I had no idea it was this late. Why didn't you call me?"

"Believe me, Fiona, we tried. Several times."

She'd turned off her phone. Her hand crept into the pocket of her overalls to turn it back on. "Sorry," she said. "Didn't hear it ring. I have a show coming up and I have a lot of work to do."

He stared down at her, and she had the uncomfortable feeling that she wasn't fooling him at all. Then he took in the barrier of boxes around the edge of the table. "Barricading yourself in your studio?" he asked.

"I'm demon-proofing it."

His eyebrows rose. "I didn't know we had a demon problem in Spruce Lake."

"Only one of them. Big, black and furry."

"Tasha?" His mouth twitched. When they were kids, a dimple in his cheek would flash when he laughed. Did he still have it?

"He's trying to stake his claim to my

studio. I'm trying to keep him off the table. I think we've reached détente. He hasn't knocked one of my gemstones onto the floor today."

"You're becoming quite the animal lover, aren't you?"

She stroked Annabelle, who'd returned to her post at Fiona's side. She'd always wanted a pet when she was younger, but her father would never allow an animal in the house. And she hadn't thought it would be fair to keep one in her New York City loft. She wasn't going to tell Jackson that, though. He probably still thought she wasn't fit to own a pet. "I don't have much choice, do I?"

"There are always choices." He sighed. "Most of the animals I have boarding will be gone in a week. If you want to bring him back, we'll have room for him. He can stay until Charlie's mom gets home."

She settled back in the chair. "I thought the reason you sent Tasha home was to irritate me. To make me mad." She gave him a cool smile. "Part of the game, right?"

His eyes gleamed. "Fun, isn't it?"

Way too much fun. But she wasn't about to tell him that. "Maybe mildly amusing. After all, there isn't a whole lot of entertainment in Spruce Lake, is there?" She smiled to herself when he scowled. "So now you want to take him back?"

"I thought you wanted to get rid of him."

Charlie would be upset if she sent Tasha to the clinic. "Why did you really send him home with Charlie, Jackson? Other than to get under my skin."

"Getting under your skin is always a worthwhile goal," he said, his dimple finally flashing. "But bottom line? Charlie needs that cat. Do you have any idea how tough this summer has been for him? He moved to a new town. He met his birth father. He got a stepfather. The kid needs a pet."

"He has his snakes."

Jackson snorted. "Yeah, they're real cuddly. And they have lots of personality, don't they?"

"Charlie seems to think so."

"Trust me. Charlie likes those snakes, but they're not the same as a dog or a cat. Charlie's feeling a little lost since his mom left on her honeymoon. He needed something to take care of."

She was unsure what to say. Jackson had *seen* Charlie. Really seen him and understood him. She should have recognized Charlie's loneliness.

Maybe Jackson was right. Maybe she *was* self-centered and self-absorbed.

"You took the time to get to know Charlie," she said. "And figure out what he needed. Thank you, Jackson."

He shrugged. "He and Lindy and Logan are at the clinic almost every day. It wasn't hard."

"Demon Cat and I came to an understanding this morning. I'm not sending him back."

His gaze was perceptive. "I know you need order in your life, Fiona. But this is just until Bree and Parker get home. Then Charlie and Tasha will be gone to their own house, and you can get on with your life. Wherever that may be."

She looked away. "I'm perfectly fine with chaos."

"Is that right?"

"Absolutely." She picked Annabelle up, and the dog licked her chin.

"Okay. You have a good time with your chaos, but you can drop Tasha off at the clinic next week if you need to."

"Thank you," she said. She met his gaze over the dog. He needed to leave so she could forget the kindness and sensitivity he'd displayed about Charlie. She hadn't wanted to know that Jackson had grown from a kind boy to a thoughtful, caring man.

Silence stretched uncomfortably long, then Jackson set a brown paper bag on her worktable. "We tried to call because the insulin I ordered didn't show up today. I should get it tomorrow, so I brought a few more doses to get you through until then."

Fiona touched the white plastic bag. "All right," she said. "Thank you for bringing it over. Sorry you had to make the trip."

"Sorry I distracted you."

His eyes darkened, and she wondered if he was remembering all the times he'd snuck into her studio and distracted her. All the things they'd done when he was here.

All the things Fiona had tried so hard to forget.

CHAPTER SEVEN

"I'LL TALK to the Philadelphia police," Helen Cherney said, making a note on a legal pad. "That's the first step. But it would be quicker to hire a private investigator to track Barb down for us."

Trying to avoid the attorney's sympathetic gaze, Fiona studied the books and diplomas lining the walls of Helen's law office and the colorful paintings alongside them. Her situation was probably depressingly familiar. But it was new and painful to Fiona. "That's a great idea, but I don't have a lot of money right now, Helen." She tried to smile and had a feeling she failed miserably. "It all disappeared. Along with Barb."

"Then we'll have to figure out a less expensive option." Helen pursed her lips and stared thoughtfully at Fiona. "I have an idea," she said slowly. "It's unusual, but it might work."

"Yeah?" Fiona looked at Helen's steady eyes and felt a stirring of hope. "Tell me."

"You know Jamie Evans, don't you?" Helen cleared her throat. "He's a Spruce Lake cop."

"I've known Jamie for years. What about him?"

"I think I could persuade him to do a little moonlighting," Helen said, her cheeks turning pink. "He knows how to run an investigation. How to track down people who don't want to be found. He loves puzzles. He'd probably do it just for a challenge."

Fiona frowned. "I don't want Jamie doing something illegal."

"Trust me. He won't. But he knows how to use all the tools a P.I. would use. And he'll work cheap."

"It sounds as if I'd be taking advantage of him," Fiona said.

Helen's eyes gleamed. "You won't be. I will. And Jamie loves it when I take advantage of him."

"Too much information, Helen." Fiona was a little jealous of the woman's glow. "But I'm happy for you and Jamie."

"Thanks," she said. "I resisted for a long time. He's younger than I am. Quite a bit younger. I thought it mattered. Now I wonder what was wrong with me." She smiled dreamily. "Sometimes, it's just right. You know?"

"Yeah, I do." Fiona tried not to think about how it used to be with Jackson. Before she dumped him. "Are you sure Jamie won't mind doing this?"

"We're having lunch together. I'll ask him." She leaned across the desk to pat Fiona's hand. "I bet it won't take him long to track Barb down. Once we know where she is, it'll be easy to have the police pick her up."

"I'm doing an important show in a month, and I really need the money for materials." She cringed at the neediness in her voice, but she was getting more nervous as the days went by without any sign of Barb.

"Jamie will get on it right away," Helen promised.

"Thank you, Helen." Fiona slapped the arm of her chair and stood. "Let me know when the retainer runs out." She hoped she'd have some of her money back from Barb by then.

"Absolutely," Helen said. "I'll keep track of my hours."

Something about Helen's tone made Fiona wonder how meticulous she'd really be. She'd have to keep track herself.

Damn Barb. This was humiliating. To wonder if she'd have enough money to pay her bill.

Helen handed her a card as she opened the door to her waiting room. "Call me anytime, Fiona."

"Take care, Helen," Fiona said, but the attorney wasn't paying any attention. A tall man with dark blond hair and green eyes wearing a dark blue police uniform tossed a magazine onto one of the chairs. "Hey, gorgeous," he said, cupping his hand around the back of Helen's head and pulling her close for a kiss.

Helen sank into him for a moment, then eased away. "Jamie, you know Fiona McInnes, don't you?"

"I sure do." Jamie grinned at her. "I haven't had any more phone calls from the Philadelphia police, so I assume you're behaving yourself."

"Bite me, Jamie."

"Sorry," he said, slinging an arm around Helen's shoulders and absently caressing her arm through her white silk blouse. "I'd be glad to oblige, but I'm into monogamy."

Helen bumped his hip with hers. "Fiona has some business I need to talk to you about at lunch."

"I thought we'd eat in your office," he said, grabbing a bag from the chair. "We'd have more time. I brought sandwiches."

Helen blushed. "Sandwiches sound great."

"More privacy here. To discuss Fiona's business," he added with a straight face.

"I'll leave you two, then," Fiona said, feeling like an intruder.

The murmur of Jamie's voice followed her out the door. It didn't sound like he was talking business.

She swung into her car, alone and lonely. Helen looked so happy. And Jamie was over the moon.

First Zoe, then Bree, and now Helen. Was everyone in this town pairing up?

She'd never been interested in a long-term relationship. Not since Jackson, anyway. She liked her life just the way it was, the way she'd struggled against all the odds to make it— focused on her art, with plenty of solitude, and any spare time devoted to her friends.

She'd had her share of dates, and even a couple of semiserious relationships since she left Spruce Lake. None of them had tempted her into anything permanent. She always assumed that she hadn't yet met "the one."

But maybe it was more than that. Maybe

there was a vital part of her lacking. Maybe she wasn't cut out to fall in love, get married, have children. Maybe she'd somehow lost that piece of herself.

Would things have been different if she hadn't walked away from Jackson? Would they have gotten married, had children?

And what if things *had* been different? Would her passion for Jackson have overpowered her passion for her art? Would she have buried those dreams inside her and left them to fester in her soul?

Would she have been content to stay in Spruce Lake, be the wife of the town veterinarian and dabble in jewelry design, rather than commit to learning her craft and being taken seriously?

No. She'd made the only decision she could have made. She'd needed to leave Spruce Lake, needed to go to New York and do everything she did to make her dream come true.

Even if, sometimes at night, she'd wished she hadn't had to choose between Jackson and her jewelry.

This wasn't the time to be brooding about her life, she told herself as she peeled away from Helen's office. Brooding wasn't going to fix what had gone wrong. Hiring Helen had been a good first step. Now she needed to spend her time working. To remember the joy she used to feel. Her sense of discovery. Her passion.

She was entirely free in her studio. It was the one place where she was fully herself.

The only way to really make this right, to really fix it, was to figure out a cure for the malaise that had been creeping over her for the past year. To figure out a way to get back the edge she'd lost.

The show at the Clybourne was the answer. She'd reinvent herself, and FeeMac jewelry. She'd finally achieve all of her goals.

She had to go home to New York as soon as Bree got back.

"We got a letter today, Aunt Fee." Charlie spoke behind her as she bent to look in the refrigerator.

"Yeah?" she said, pushing aside a bag of lettuce as she searched for the leftover spaghetti sauce. They hadn't used it, had they? "From your mom? Is she having a great time in Hawaii?"

"No, not from my mom." Charlie cleared his throat, and Fiona heard the nerves in his voice. "From the, uh, Spruce Lake Park District."

Fiona turned around. "Why is the Park District writing to us?"

"Remember I signed up for that basketball league? The one that's supposed to get kids ready to play in junior high and high school?"

"Vaguely." She had absolutely no recollection of it.

"It was right before Mom and Parker got married." Charlie swallowed. "On the form, there was a place to have a parent sign up to volunteer. So I signed you up."

"You did what?" Fiona closed the refrigerator door.

"I said you'd volunteer to help the team. I couldn't sign up unless a parent volunteered, and I really want to play basketball this winter." The words spilled out of Charlie in a pleading torrent.

"I thought you were doing cross-country."

"That's in the fall. This is after cross-country."

"Did your mom say you could play basketball? Is it okay with your doctor?"

"There's nothing wrong with my heart anymore," Charlie said heatedly. "Mom asked the cardiologist about cross-country, and she said it was fine. There's less running in basketball than in cross-country."

"Okay, so you're cleared to play. Back to the 'signing me up' part. What did you sign me up for?"

"You don't sign up for specific stuff. You just had to say that a parent or other responsible adult would help out the team." He grinned at her. "You're responsible, aren't you, Aunt Fee?"

"I might be responsible for some serious whining," she said, "depending on what I'm supposed to do."

Charlie rubbed the paper between his thumb and forefinger. "I had to list your skills."

"So did you tell them I'd make jewelry for everyone?" she asked. "Because I could do that."

"Skills that could help the team, I mean." The paper fluttered from Charlie's hand and he bent to pick it up. His voice was muffled as he said something to the floor.

"What did you say?"

Charlie straightened. "I told them you played basketball in college," he repeated. "I remember my mom talking about it. How you were such a hotshot that you walked onto your college team."

"I was hardly a hotshot. And it was a long time ago, Charlie. I haven't played in years."

Jackson had taught her. He'd been a star in high school, and she'd gone to every game. When he showed her how to dribble, how to shoot, how to defend, he'd said she was a natural.

When she'd gone away to study jewelry design, she'd continued to play. She'd been pretty good. When she realized she'd done it to stay connected, in some small way, to Jackson, she'd quit the team.

"But you did play at that design school," he said doggedly. "And that's what I put on the sign-up sheet."

"Okay. Give me the bad news. What do they have me doing? Keeping statistics for the team? Organizing the parent treats?"

"Why is it bad news?" Charlie said. "I thought it would be a nice nephew-aunt bonding thing."

Fiona's lips twitched. "You're a smart kid. Sometimes I hate that you're so smart. So what's my job?"

"You're the assistant coach."

She sank into a seat at the kitchen table. "Assistant coach? I don't know how to do that."

"Sure you do, Aunt Fee." He was clearly relieved she hadn't lost her temper. "You know how to play. You just have to teach *us* how to play. It's simple."

"Yeah. Simple." She had a career to resuscitate and an embezzler to find. And a move back to New York to orchestrate. "Why didn't you ask your dad to do this? I don't want to edge him out. He would probably love spending the time with you."

"Nice try, but Ted is a total dork when it comes to sports. He doesn't even care about the Packers! He probably doesn't know what a basketball looks like."

"What about your aunt Zoe?" She was grasping at straws, but she was desperate. "She's into sports. She'd probably like some nephew-aunt bonding."

"Right," he scoffed. "I can just see her on the court. She'd confuse the guys—they'd think she hid the basketball under her shirt. Pregnant women can't be coaches."

"Is there a rule about that? Because I never heard that rule."

"Please, Aunt Fee?" he said, and his voice was quieter. Completely serious. "I want to learn how to play basketball. I want to be on this team. A bunch of guys from school are on it. You'd have fun. We wouldn't give you a hard time or anything."

"I know you wouldn't, Charlie." She wrapped her arm around his shoulder and hugged him, touched. "And if you did, it would be a sad day when I couldn't handle a bunch of twelve-year-old punks."

"You think you're pretty tough, don't you?" he said, punching her lightly on the shoulder.

"You have no idea, kid," she said as she let him go. "Anyone on the team I know besides you?"

Charlie nodded. "You know Logan. He's on the team."

"Logan?" Oh, no. "So who's the coach, Charlie?"

"That's the best part," he said happily. "Dr. Grant is the coach."

CHAPTER EIGHT

"PLEASE, ZOE. You have to do this for me." Fiona was begging, but she didn't care. "I can't coach that basketball team."

"Why not?" Her sister leaned back in her creaky desk chair. Although Zoe was identical to Fiona—except for the hair—she looked softer now. Her face was fuller, her expression more gentle than Fiona had ever seen.

Happiness had softened her sister.

Add in a pregnancy, and Zoe was a puddle of sloppy sentimentality.

Which was why Fiona thought it would be easy to convince her sister to take over the job as assistant coach of Charlie's team. But Zoe was proving that the steel in her spine hadn't completely dissolved.

"I just can't," Fiona said. "You know what's going on with Barb. How she disappeared with all my money. I have a show in less than a month, and I have to make new pieces for it."

"Are you really going to be working 24/7, Fee?" Zoe's eyes narrowed. "You can't take a few hours a week to do something I know you're good at?"

"I haven't played basketball in years," Fiona said desperately.

"Didn't sound like they were asking you to play. They're asking you to teach a bunch of kids how to play." Zoe straightened in her chair. Although she was only a couple of months along, she already had a visible baby bump.

"There are reasons I don't want to do it," Fiona said, pacing Zoe's cramped office. "Good reasons."

"Such as…?"

"It's complicated, Zo," Fiona said, jamming her hands through her hair.

Zoe pushed a pile of papers away from the center of her desk and studied her appointment calendar. The Safe Harbor Women's Shelter was her life…or at least it used to be until Gideon swept her off her feet. "I have plenty of time," she said, folding her hands on top of her stomach. "So tell me about the complications."

That would mean she'd have to confide in Zoe. She'd never shared the details of her life with her sisters. When they were younger, self-preservation had required secrecy—their difficult father had delighted in pitting one triplet against the other.

All of them had had secrets they'd hidden.

And after she'd escaped to New York, she'd seemed so far removed from Zoe and Bree. She'd felt like a separate person for the first time in her life, and she'd relished the freedom.

But in the five months she'd been home in Spruce Lake, she'd grown closer to both of her sisters. They'd worked together to clean out their father's house and get it ready for Bree and Parker to move in. Zoe and Bree had confided in her when they'd fallen in love, then cried on her shoulder when everything had gone wrong.

She took a deep breath.

"I don't want to do it because of who I'd be coaching with," she finally said. She fiddled with the pins on Zoe's corkboard, unwilling to look at her sister.

"Shooter Clemmins?" Zoe asked with a grin. Fiona and Shooter had been sworn enemies in high school.

"I wish it was Shooter," Fiona said, turning around. "I could handle him."

The smile fell away from Zoe's face. "Who is it, Fee? I can't imagine anyone you'd clash with more than Shooter."

"Jackson Grant," Fiona said, flopping into one of the chairs in front of Zoe's desk.

"Jackson?" Zoe frowned. "What's wrong with him? He's a great guy."

Fiona swung the desk chair back and forth. "I know Jackson. Knew him, anyway. We dated through high school."

"You what?" Zoe shot to her feet.

"You heard me. We hung out. Dated. Went steady. However you want to put it." She nudged at a soup can that held pens and pencils. It was decorated with childish drawings on a piece of colored construction paper. "You must have heard Dad yelling about that no-good Grant kid."

"I mostly put on my headphones and listened to my CD player when he started yelling." Zoe looked at Fiona, regret in her eyes. "We knew how to keep secrets, didn't we?"

"We had it down to an art form."

"So why don't you want to coach with him? It would be a chance to reconnect."

"Believe me, Zo, we've already reconnected." She told her sister about Annabelle, about the tantrum in their dad's home office, about Lindy. "It would be too awkward to work with him, especially after what I did to him."

"What did you do?" Zoe asked quietly.

"He wanted to get married, but I just wanted to escape Spruce Lake. To go to design school, go to New York and become a famous jewelry designer. And I couldn't do that in Spruce Lake."

Zoe came around the desk and sat on it in front of her. "So what happened?"

"I told him we were through and walked away. I was sad about it for a long time, although I knew I'd done the right thing. For me. I needed New York…everything I couldn't have here. In the same town as Dad." A lump swelled in her throat. "A year later, I found out he'd gotten some girl at college pregnant less than a month after I broke up with him. Mallory. The one he married. It sure didn't take him long to get over me."

"And now you're supposed to be his assistant coach."

"Not if *you* can do it. Think of all the time you'll get to spend with Charlie."

"I'd love to have more Charlie time, but I can't do it." Zoe took Fiona's hand. "I have some news, Fee. I was going to wait until Bree and Parker got home and tell you together, but it's why I can't do the basketball thing."

"Is something wrong? With the munchkin?" Fiona grabbed Zoe when her sister hesitated.

"No, the babies are fine. We're having twins," she said. Her face glowed with joy. "Gideon and I had an ultrasound a couple of days ago. So even if I wanted to do it for you, my doctor wouldn't let me."

"Twins?" Fiona leaped up to embrace her sister. "Oh, Zo, I'm so happy for you." She put her hand on Zoe's slightly protruding belly. "Twins. Wow! I guess litters run in the family."

Zoe snorted. "I guess they do." She patted Fiona's abdomen. "One day it'll be your turn to have a litter."

"You have to have an actual relationship first," she answered. "How are you feeling?"

"I'm getting better." Zoe grimaced. "I'm still having morning sickness, but it's improving."

"What? You're sick? How come you didn't tell us?"

"I do my puking in private," Zoe said. "I didn't want you to worry."

Fiona brushed Zoe's wavy black hair away from her face. Hair with no hint of pink at the tips. "You should have told me. I'd have brought you weak tea and saltines."

"That's Gideon's job," Zoe answered. "He's gotten to be an expert at it, too. That's why I didn't tell you—I knew you'd fuss. I was too happy to put up with fussing."

"Do you know if they're boys or girls?"

"We told the doctor we didn't want to know." Zoe rubbed her stomach. "Maybe we'll break down and ask when we start to put a nursery together, but right now, Gideon and I want to be surprised."

"You must be feeling overwhelmed." She sure would have been, if she found out she was having twins.

"A little. But we have a lot of time to get used to the idea." Zoe eased off the desk and went back to her chair. "Sorry I can't help with the basketball. What about Ted? Why doesn't Charlie ask him?"

Fiona explained why Charlie hadn't asked his father, then sighed. "It'll just be for a couple of weeks, but I don't even want to do that."

"A couple of weeks? That's a short basketball season."

"That's when Bree gets home. And I go back to New York."

Zoe stilled. "You're leaving?"

"I live there, Zo. Of course I'm going back." She ignored the tiny pang in her heart. She'd miss her family more than she'd ever have guessed.

"You seem like a part of Spruce Lake now," Zoe said quietly. "Like you belong here. Things have been so good that I haven't thought about you leaving."

"I'm not going to stay away this time," Fiona promised. "I'll come home a lot." She squeezed her sister's shoulder. "I'll have nephews—and maybe nieces, too—to visit."

"It's not the same as having you in town."

"I'll pick a few fights before I leave," Fiona said, trying to smile. "Then you can be glad I'm gone."

"What's the big rush, Fee?"

"As I said, I'm having a show at a big gallery in Manhattan, and I have to get ready for it. That's the big rush. My career is in the toilet," Fiona said bluntly. "I have to resuscitate it."

"What?" Zoe sat up straight. "But you're a celebrity. You've made it."

"Not so much. Orders aren't coming in. There was an article in an important art review magazine saying my designs aren't relevant anymore." Fiona shook her head. "Even a twelve-year-old kid said FeeMac jewelry was stupid."

"Like a kid would know," Zoe scoffed. "Who was the brat, anyway?"

"Jackson's daughter, Lindy."

"Are you kidding me? Lindy said that? She's a sweetheart."

"That sweetheart has an evil twin, and it isn't Logan. If she's been pleasant to you, it's because she didn't think you were scheming to get your claws into her father."

"Oh my God." Zoe tried to hide her smile. "Lindy thinks you're after Jackson, and meanwhile you're running back to New York to get away from him. This could be fun."

"You're not being helpful, Zo," Fiona said. She didn't want to be, but she was amused herself. A few months ago, this conversation would have made her flee Zoe's office. Their relationship was changing. Improving.

"Are you interested in Jackson?" Zoe asked, taking Fiona's hand. "Truth?"

Fiona looked down at Zoe's hand holding hers. The diamonds in her wedding ring flashed in the sunlight and made her eyes water. "Truth, I'm still attracted to him. Physically, anyway. We had…we were…" She sighed. "The sex was amazing, Zo. Neither of us knew what we were doing, and it was still incredible. It's hard to forget something like that."

"And you're not interested in round two?"

"Nothing's changed for me, Zoe. My career

is still as important as it ever was. More, I think. With everything that's going wrong."

"That didn't sound like a no to me." Fiona heard a car stop in front of the shelter. Zoe glanced out the window and stood. "The police are here, and that usually means they've brought me a domestic violence victim. I have to go, Fee." She hugged her sister. "You can suck it up and coach for a couple of weeks, can't you?"

"It's either that or disappoint Charlie. I'm not going to do that."

"Good luck, then," Zoe said. She gave her sister a sly grin. "I'll be waiting for reports."

"Seventh-grade basketball games are pretty boring."

"Oh, I don't think these particular games will be boring. Not if you play them the right way."

"I'm leaving," Fiona said, but she couldn't suppress a tiny smile. "I don't think my nieces or nephews should be hearing this kind of talk."

"WHAT THE HECK." Jackson stared at the letter he'd just opened. "I don't believe it."

"What don't you believe, Dad?" Lindy asked as she set the table for dinner. Technically, they didn't really need to set the table for take-out fried chicken. But it made it seem more like a real meal if they used dishes and silverware.

He glanced over at his daughter, who watched him with a worried expression. "Nothing, baby. Just something about Logan's basketball team."

"You're still coaching my team, aren't you?"

"Of course I am, Lind. I'm coaching both of your teams." He'd signed up to be the assistant coach for both, but the park district had made him the head coach. How the hell did they think he was going to do that? He waved the letter. "This was just confirming it." And letting him know his assistant coach for Logan's team was Fiona. Talk about fate biting you in the ass. Or maybe it was karma. Either way, he'd been nailed.

Had Fiona deliberately arranged it?

A little more payback?

Jerking his chain like he'd jerked hers with the cat?

Jackson smiled as he stared at her name in the letter. If she wanted to play games, he'd be happy to oblige her.

Bring it on, Fee.

"Charlie better be on my team," Logan

said, interrupting his thoughts. "Or we're going to be majorly pissed off."

"He is. And watch your mouth, Logan." Jackson folded the letter. "You know the rules about language."

"You swore when you read that letter," Logan pointed out.

"I did not." He'd caught himself just in time.

"When's our first practice?" Lindy asked.

"Uh, not sure, Lind," he said. "I have to call my assistant coach and see when he can make it."

"How about mine?" Logan asked.

"Same thing." He put the letter on the counter. That was going to be an interesting phone call.

CHAPTER NINE

THE DOOR OF THE Lake House opened, letting in a blast of hot August air, as Fiona walked in. She scanned the room, spotted him near the big window overlooking the water and headed his way.

She wasn't wearing overalls. She wore a white skirt that floated around her legs when she walked, and a dark blue shirt cut low in the front. Her necklace was all angles and lines of silver, with only a couple of small stones. Not her usual design—and it was a little alarming that he knew enough about her jewelry to know it wasn't typical FeeMac.

Clearly, he'd spent too much time searching her on the Internet.

"Hello, Fiona." He stood as she neared the table and pulled out a chair for her. "Thanks for meeting me."

"We needed to talk." She adjusted the

pendant on its chain and smoothed the shirt. Then she shifted in her chair.

"What's wrong?" he asked.

She stilled, then folded her hands on the table.

"I have a lot on my plate right now." He thought he saw a hint of desperation in her eyes, but then it was gone. "Just like you, I'm sure." She rubbed her shoulders. "It's freezing in here."

She'd always been slick about changing the subject when she didn't want to talk about something. "Yeah, they have the temperature set pretty low." Although he didn't allow his gaze to drop, the thin material of her shirt couldn't hide her tight nipples. God bless air-conditioning. "You want me to find you a jacket?"

"No, thanks. I want to know what we're going to do about this coaching thing," she said briskly. "I'm sure you're not happy about it, either."

"Why do you say that?"

She leveled her gaze at him. "Can you honestly say you want to spend time with me? Twice a week, plus the games?"

No, he didn't. "You don't sound very happy about it, either."

"I have a lot to do in the next few weeks." She touched the necklace. "But I'm determined to be there for Charlie."

"And I need the help. I'm coaching both Logan and Lindy's teams. So I guess we're stuck with each other."

"That's one way of putting it."

"How else should I put it? I have no idea what you're bringing to the table." Other than trouble. That was a given, if he spent that much time with her.

Her eyes narrowed. "Exactly which table are you talking about?"

"Coaching, of course." He took a drink of beer. "How much do you remember about basketball?"

"Enough to coach a bunch of eleven- and twelve-year-olds." Her fingers slid over her necklace, and he caught himself staring at her hand.

"You afraid I'm going to say or do something inappropriate, like arguing with you instead of coaching the kids?" he said, trying to regroup.

"You? Inappropriate?" Fiona smiled and leaned forward. "I'm sure you'll be the model of decorum."

He struggled to keep his gaze from

dropping. "I'll be on my best behavior. As long as you play fair."

"I always play fair," she said.

The waitress approached, and Fiona sat up and smiled at her. "I'd like a glass of cabernet, please."

"Sure thing." Sandy glanced at him. "You okay there, Jackson?"

Hell, no, he wasn't okay. She'd turned his tactics back on him, and he wasn't sure if he was amused or turned on. Or both.

"I'm good, Sandy. Thanks." He was so far from good, it was scary.

Fiona leaned back against the wooden chair, a glint of amusement in her eyes. "So, Jackson, what are we going to do about the situation?"

He sprawled in his own chair, waited.

She raised her eyebrows. "If we do this, our past isn't part of it. You don't pick a fight with me in front of the kids. You don't goad me into losing my temper."

"Is that still easy to do?"

"I'm twenty-nine years old," she said. "I know how to control myself."

"That's too bad." He set his beer on the table and stared at her.

Her hand tightened on the wineglass and she took a deep breath. "I didn't come here to…"

She traced the stem of the wineglass, and he couldn't tear his gaze away.

Damn it. He was being stupid. "Maybe we should talk about the past."

Her finger stilled, then she centered the glass in front of her. "Is that necessary?"

"It might clear the air. Before we spend all this time together coaching."

"We're not sharing our life histories with these kids," she said in the cool, impersonal voice she'd perfected long ago. "All we're sharing is basketball."

It would be damn hard to forget their past when every time he watched her dribble a basketball, he'd remember the hours they'd spent together, playing. Bumping each other. Wrestling for the basketball.

And how their games usually ended.

He wasn't going to let himself go down that path again.

"Tell me this, Fiona. What did you think would happen when you signed up to be assistant coach? Who did you think you were going to be working with?"

She shredded a piece of the cocktail napkin. "Are you suggesting that I signed up specifically to be your assistant coach? That I knew who'd be coaching the team?"

"Charlie knew I'd be the coach."

"Charlie didn't share that with me. In fact, I had no idea he'd signed me up for anything."

"So why did you agree?" Had he really thought she'd had an ulterior motive for signing up to coach?

"Sorry to disillusion you, but I didn't want to disappoint Charlie. This is about my nephew. Not you." She patted his hand. "You'll recover, though."

"Yeah, I did before, didn't I?" He drained his beer and signaled Sandy for another pint.

She stiffened. "We both did, didn't we? And it wasn't nearly as hard as either one of us thought it would be."

The silence stretched uncomfortably long. Finally, her gaze dropped to his beer glass. He had no trouble reading her mind. When they were kids, he'd sworn he'd never drink. Now he'd drained one beer and asked for another. "No, I'm not turning into my old man. I know my damn limits."

She nodded slowly. "I can see that."

"Trust me. If I was going to take up drinking, it would have been during my marriage." He pushed the Guinness to one side. "You don't have to worry that I'll show up drunk at practices."

"That's not what I was thinking."

"No? Then what *were* you thinking?"

"I was wondering what happened to your marriage."

She was what had happened to his marriage. The nine-hundred-pound gorilla that had shared the bed with him and Mallory. "The usual. We grew apart. Isn't that the polite thing to say?"

"I don't know. I've never been married."

"No? Ever tempted?"

"Once." She took a sip of wine. Her hand trembled slightly when she set it on the table.

"What happened?"

"The timing wasn't right. We wanted different things." She wouldn't look at him. "The usual."

"Anyone I know?" He gripped his beer in his suddenly sweaty hand.

"Yes. A long time ago." Before he could say anything, she folded her hands on the table. "Is this going to work?"

"Is what going to work?"

"The coaching. Can we work together, in spite of your why-I-don't-want-to-work-with-Fiona list?"

If he was smart, he'd put one of those together, ASAP. "You want to be there for

Charlie. I need to coach my kids' teams—apparently no other parent was stupid enough to admit they know how to play this bloody game! My kids have had a rough time, and we need to do some normal things together. So I guess you and I don't have a choice."

Her lower lip turned all pouty. He quickly took a drink of beer.

"I can do anything for a couple of weeks," she finally said. "Even work with you."

"Nice. But it's a lot more than two weeks. The league goes until the middle of October, when they have tryouts for the school teams."

"Then Bree or Parker will have to do it. I'm going back to New York."

"In two weeks?" He hoped his surprise didn't show.

"Or less. I have a show coming up at a gallery in Manhattan. A crucial show. I promised Bree I'd stay and watch Charlie while she was on her honeymoon. But when she and Parker get back, I'm gone."

He should be happy to hear that. Once she left, he'd forget about her again. Life would be simpler. It would certainly make life with Lindy easier. "So you're running away again?"

Instead of bristling, as he expected, her expression softened. "No. I'm going back home.

To my job. My life. I didn't want to come to Spruce Lake. I didn't want anything to do with the memories here, although it's been wonderful to reconnect with Zoe and Bree and get to know Charlie. I still hate that damn house. Can't get out of there soon enough."

The idea of Fiona having a life—a home—that had nothing to do with Spruce Lake still hurt him. And the image of her as a successful businesswoman…well, he just couldn't rationalize that with the artist in front of him. The way she'd drift off in the middle of a conversation when she got an idea, the way it was almost impossible to get her attention when she was working, the designs she scribbled constantly in the notebook she always carried.

He'd never thought of her as the type to run a business. But that's what she did. And from everything he'd read, she did it very well.

"Tell me how it feels to be a celebrity. What it's like to run a national company."

She twirled the wineglass by the stem, staring into the red depths. Finally she looked up. "Are you really interested?"

"Tell me."

FIONA'S HEART TRIPPED when she saw the sincerity in his eyes. Jackson had always been able to make her feel as if no one else existed. As if she was the only person who mattered at all.

And suddenly she wanted to talk about the whole mess. To share it with Jackson.

She took a long drink, then centered the wine on the table in front of her again. "My business manager took off with all my money. My agent didn't have time to deal with it because I'm a small fish in his pond, so I fired him. But not before he told me that my designs were stale and outdated. Bottom line, my 'company' has one foot in the grave and the other on a banana peel."

"What?" He straightened in the chair, pushing the Guinness aside. "When did all this happen?"

"I found out about the money and had the illuminating conversation with my agent that day you came looking for me."

"That's why you had that meltdown in your old man's office."

"I was angry, Jackson." Fiona finished her wine. She should have guessed he'd ask about that. The memory still made her shudder. "I was venting, and you caught me."

Sandy appeared at the table. "Another cabernet?"

"Yes, please," Fiona answered. She needed something to do with her hands, even though she needed to keep her wits while she was with Jackson. He was as quick as he'd always been.

"What's this crap about your designs being outdated?" Jackson said.

Jackson had always told her she was brilliant. Her throat swelled, but she said, "Are you sure you want to hear the ugly details?"

"Someone else's problems are always more interesting than your own."

He surprised a tiny laugh out of her. "Isn't that the truth?" All the details spilled out of her—her dissatisfaction with her designs recently, her agent's advice to keep doing the same thing and his subsequent dismissal of her work.

"No wonder you looked as if someone had slapped you when Lindy made that crack the other day about your jewelry," he said. He touched her hand briefly. "She didn't mean it, you know. She pestered me for a solid month to take her to your show at Pieces. And she wears the earrings almost every day."

"I know," she said quietly. "I understand she feels threatened by me. She was just striking out, hoping to hurt me."

"She's a good kid, Fiona."

"I guess I bring out the worst in her."

"Any woman I look at brings that out," he said with a sigh.

"Must make it hard to date." She kept her voice carefully neutral.

"I'm not interested in dating. I have enough on my hands with the kids and the clinic."

"Lindy made it sound as if women were chasing you through the streets of Spruce Lake."

He frowned. "I don't know why. I haven't gone on a date since they started living here with me."

"Haven't they always lived here with you?"

"Mallory and I used to share custody. They spent their summers and one weekend a month in Spruce Lake. They moved here seven months ago."

She waited for him to explain, but he didn't. That was fine with her. She didn't want to discuss his marriage, either.

She caught the waitress's eye—Sandy's—and signaled for the check. "So are we good with the coaching?"

He nodded, but she couldn't read his expression. "We're good with the coaching. I've got the junior high gym reserved for

Tuesdays and Thursdays at five for the boys' practice. Does that work for you?"

"I'll make sure it does."

Sandy set the check down, and Fiona put a couple of bills on the table. Jackson raised his eyebrows and slipped his own cash into the folder. "Put your money away, Fiona."

"I always pay my own way," she said coolly.

"Is that right?" He handed the folder to Sandy, who nodded her thanks and disappeared fast, knowing an argument when she saw one. Jackson pushed Fiona's money back to her. "I don't let women pay their way when they're out with me."

"We weren't 'out,'" she said, ignoring the butterflies in her stomach.

"No?" He stood and helped her with her chair, then, despite her resistance, opened the door for her. "That's funny, I thought we were sitting at the same table. I thought we were talking to each other. Did I miss something?"

She headed for the parking lot in back of the Lake House. "This was a business meeting, Jackson. Nothing more." She reached Bree's old Honda and turned to face him. "I'll see you on Tuesday."

Before she could lift the handle, Jackson put his hand over hers. "Business, Fee?"

"Of course." Her heart began to pound, but she turned to face him. "What else would it be?"

CHAPTER TEN

JACKSON STARED down at her. When she tried to shift away, his body shifted with hers.

She should have known he'd kiss her. She'd seen it in his eyes as they'd talked—the awareness, the slow build of heat, the desire she knew too well.

She felt the metal of her sister's car against her back and the heat of his body against her front. Then his lips brushed hers.

His scent, the spicy aftershave he still used and the clean smell of soap and fresh air. The way he gripped her shoulders, as if he'd never let go. The shape of his body, familiar even after so long.

The way he tasted, the distinctive flavor of Jackson identifiable even beneath the dark tang of the beer.

She remembered Jackson far too well, although it had been so long since she'd touched him.

His arms went around her as he deepened the kiss, consuming her.

Her legs trembled, and he swung her around into a pool of darkness beneath the old oak tree beside the car at the edge of the parking lot. He pressed her back against the rough bark.

Her plunge into need and passion was like a steep drop on a roller coaster. Everything faded away until there was only Jackson. The feel of his callused hands touching her face. The hard length of his body, touching hers from chest to knee. The evidence of his desire, touching her stomach.

"Fee," he groaned, trailing his mouth down her neck to her collarbone. "It's been so long. I haven't forgotten anything." He put his palm on her chest, traced the cool metal of her pendant, then cupped her breast. "Not a damn thing."

Putting her hand over his, she said, "Neither have I."

The sound of laughter and the slam of a car door drifted across the parking lot and, without taking his mouth off hers, Jackson shifted. To keep her hidden, she realized, and sanity returned with a rush.

"I can't do this," she whispered.

"Neither can I." He nipped at the tendon in her throat, and she clenched his shoulders.

"We have to stop." She put her hands on his chest to create some distance between their bodies.

"Yeah, this is a really bad idea." He found her mouth again with a desperation that said he'd die if he didn't kiss her. "We'll stop in just a minute," he murmured against her lips. "I've dreamed about you, Fee."

God help her, she'd dreamed about him, too. The hard contours of his body touched her breasts, her hips, her thighs. Reality was far more powerful than her memory. "We're asking for trouble."

He shifted and his body pressed a little harder. "As I remember it, that never stopped either of us before."

"We're not kids anymore, Jackson. We should have more self-control."

"I do. I haven't lost control in years." He lifted her hand and kissed her palm.

She shivered but didn't pull her hand away. Her body ached for him and her mouth was greedy for his. Desire she hadn't felt in a very long time beat a slow, hard rhythm in her blood.

"This would be a huge mistake," she whispered. "I don't want this, and neither do you."

"You're right." Their hands were still joined, and he tugged her closer until her hands were trapped between their bodies. She flexed her fingers, savoring his heat and the hard muscles of his chest. He shuddered and swept a hand down her back.

If they hadn't been in public, they would have had each other's clothes off by now.

The realization was enough to send a chill through her. She'd worked so hard to get beyond Jackson. To relegate him to a memory. Now, one kiss and she was ready to jump into bed with him.

The upheavals in her business and her own uncertainties about her work must really be affecting her. Making her vulnerable and unsure of herself.

She pushed him away, and her pendant caught on his shirt and broke. Silver gleamed in the dim light, and he untangled it from his shirt.

Moonlight filtered through the trees, dappling his face and hiding his eyes. "Fee." He stared at the broken jewelry for a long moment, then touched it to the fragment still hanging from the chain around her neck. "You used to lose control on a regular basis. Does that ever happen anymore?"

"No." She couldn't afford to lose control. If she did, everything would come tumbling down. She took the piece of the pendant out of his hand. "I'll see you Tuesday, Jackson."

The metal cooled in her hand as she walked to her car. As she pulled away, he was still standing beneath the tree.

THE DOOR OF THE GYM opened behind Jackson as he was trying to explain a drill to the girls gathered around him. Half of his attention was on the group of boys at the other end of the court, who were now throwing basketballs at one another instead of at the baskets.

He ignored both groups as he watched Fiona walk in. The pink streaks in her hair were brighter today. A pair of running shorts emphasized her long, toned legs and a T-shirt clung to her breasts and hips. Sensible clothes for playing basketball.

His mouth went dry.

One of the boy's basketballs hit him in the back. "Knock it off!" he yelled at the boys. "You're supposed to be practicing free throws. Don't make me come down there."

My God. When had he become his father?

He turned back to the girls in time to see pint-size Samantha Peters roll her eyes. "You have something you want to say, Sam?" he asked.

"Boys," she said, rolling her eyes again. "They're so immature."

"Aren't you afraid your eyes will fall out if you keep doing that?"

Giggles erupted from all ten of the girls. As he waited for them to settle down, he didn't allow himself to look at Fiona. But he knew exactly where she was. "All right, let's go over this drill one more time."

Lindy, Logan, I hope you appreciate this, he thought as he watched the girls do a layup drill. Because right now, this was not fun. Working with junior high kids was like herding cats. You didn't get anywhere and you always knew they were laughing at you.

He turned to yell at the boys again and saw Fiona drop her purse onto the bleachers. She sauntered toward him.

Working together, he reminded himself. Trying to teach these kids the fundamentals of basketball. Eleven- and twelve-year-olds noticed everything. He didn't want them to notice the way he looked at their assistant coach.

He didn't want Fiona to notice, either.

"You girls practice shooting for a while,"

he said, as Fiona closed in. The boys had stopped bouncing the basketballs off one another to watch her. Timmy Kruger nudged Charlie and said something. Charlie scowled.

Timmy had always been precocious. He'd have to keep an eye on that kid.

"Hey, Fiona."

"Hello, Jackson."

She picked up a basketball and started dribbling. "Sorry I'm late," she said. "I had to make a phone call. Thanks for picking Charlie up."

"My pleasure." He hesitated as he noticed the tension in her shoulders. "Problems?"

"I don't know. Maybe." She rolled her shoulders. "Now's not the time to talk about it. What are we doing here?"

"I want to show them how to do layups. You know how to do that drill, don't you?"

"Sure."

He glanced at the girls at the other end of the gym. They were waving their hands and yelling. "Damn it." He took Fiona's arm and drew her away from the boys.

"Listen, I know you signed up to help with Charlie's team, but could you run the girls' practice today? They're driving me nuts. They weren't supposed to be on the same day, but today I didn't have a choice." He shoved his hand through his hair. "I had to cancel the girls' practice yesterday because I had an emergency at the clinic." He glanced from the girls to the boys. The girls were still arguing, and the boys were chasing one another and tripping over the basketballs on the floor.

"Where's the assistant coach for Lindy's team?"

"He's out of town today."

"Lindy isn't going to be happy."

"Lindy's going to have to suck it up," he said, a little too sharply. "It makes sense for each of us to take one group, and I pick you for the girls. Maybe they'll relate better to a woman. You know how their minds work." He shook his head. "Rachel refused to play with the red, white and blue ball. She said it was stupid."

"Clearly a young woman with a strong fashion sense."

"Oh, you're a barrel of laughs." One of the girls flounced away from the others. "Let's see if you're still smiling after an hour with that bunch."

She grinned. "Jackson, I do believe you're desperate. I like a desperate man. You can get anything you want from him."

They were in the middle of a school gym that smelled faintly of old socks and mildew, surrounded by twenty preteens. He had the beginnings of a headache pounding at his temples. And her smart-mouthed remark erased everything but Fiona from his mind.

They stared at each other for a long moment, then she picked up a ball and started dribbling. "Drills for the girls, too?"

"Yeah." He rubbed his hand over his face. "Then have them practice shooting."

"Got it."

She headed for the girls and he watched for a moment before turning back to the boys. "All right, guys, that's enough. Or do I have to start kicking some butts?"

LINDY STOOD at the front of the group, scowling, her arms crossed over her chest.

"Hi there, ladies," Fiona said. She picked up the ball she'd been dribbling and tucked it beneath her arm. "I'm Fiona McInnes. I'm going to run your practice today."

"My dad is our coach," Lindy interrupted.

"Yes, he is, Lindy," she said with a smile. "I'm just filling in for him."

A short girl with straight blond hair said, "Are you Dr. Grant's girlfriend?"

"No," Fiona said, avoiding Lindy's gaze. "I'm Charlie McInnes's aunt. And you are…?"

"Sam Peters."

"Good to meet you, Sam. Why don't the rest of you introduce yourselves?"

One girl tossed her dark brown ponytail over her shoulder. "I'm Rachel Evans. Charlie's in my social studies class. He's, like, hot."

"Thanks for sharing, Rachel." Fiona suppressed a shudder. "What about the rest of you?"

After she'd gotten all the girls' names, she said, "We're going to do a layup drill. Do you all know how to do layups?"

Most of the girls looked confused. Lindy stood to the side, scowling. "Okay," Fiona said. "Let's demonstrate. Lindy. Do you know how to do this?"

"Duh. My dad's the coach. Of course I do."

"Then guard me."

Fiona started thirty feet away from the basket, dribbling the ball. Was Jackson watching? She hoped not. It had been a long time since she played basketball.

Lindy stepped in front of her, arms waving, batting at the ball, and Fiona forced herself to pay attention. She tried to dribble past Lindy, and the girl gave her a hard hip check.

"Nice move," Fiona said.

"You're not supposed to be here." Lindy lunged for the ball again, and Fiona side-stepped her and headed for the basket. Lindy caught up quickly.

"Actually, I *am* supposed to be here," Fiona said as she dribbled in place. "I'm the assistant coach for Charlie's team."

"Then go coach the boys." She put one hand in Fiona's face and swiped at the ball with the other. Fiona barely managed to hold on to it.

"Do you think I want to do this? That I want to deal with your attitude?" Fiona bounced the ball too hard, and it flew up past her shoulder. "I signed up to coach so I could spend time with Charlie, not a snotty kid who hates me for no reason."

Lindy's arms dropped and she took a step away from Fiona. "You're not supposed to speak like that to me."

"Why is that, Lindy?" The ball hit the floor with a steady beat. "You're behaving badly, so why can't I point it out?"

"You're not my dad. Or my mom."

"Would they approve of the way you're acting?"

Lindy glanced over Fiona's shoulder. Probably looking at Jackson. "I'm going to tell my mom about you. She wouldn't like you."

"That's okay." Fiona thought about what Jackson had said the other night about his marriage. She wouldn't like Mallory, either. "I don't really care what your mom thinks of me."

Lindy continued staring at her father, as if she was willing him to come and save her from Fiona. "You're making this hard for him, you know."

"What are you talking about?" Lindy tried to sound tough, but Fiona heard the wariness in her voice.

"Your dad signed up to help coach your team and Logan's. It's great he wanted to do that, but now he's the head coach and that takes a lot of time. He had to cancel your practice yesterday because he had an emergency at the clinic." She took a cautious step to the side. Lindy followed.

"I know that." The girl's voice dripped scorn. "He tells us everything."

Fiona was very sure he didn't. "So how did you expect him to coach both your team and Logan's today?"

"He could tell us what to do and we'd do it. We don't need you."

"Sounds to me like he did tell you," Fiona said mildly. "But you were arguing instead of doing it."

"Jeannie doesn't like Rachel," Lindy muttered, kicking at the ball.

"Your dad's going to worry if he doesn't see you guys practicing." Fiona softened her voice as she moved around Lindy with the ball. "Did he have a hard day at the clinic today?" She'd noticed the lines next to his mouth and the weariness in his eyes.

"Mrs. Samuelson brought in her Chihuahua. She thought Cha Cha was pregnant, but she was really sick," Lindy said. "Dad had to do surgery on her. A lot of people had to wait. He didn't get any lunch."

"Sounds like a really bad day. Don't you want to help him out and make him feel better?"

Lindy looked at her, then over her shoulder. Fiona saw the struggle in the girl's eyes.

Jackson was watching them. Fiona knew it, even though she couldn't see him. She glanced behind her, and Lindy knocked the ball away from her.

Fiona lunged after it and fell to the floor,

smashing her elbow on the wood. She slowly got to her feet. Lindy was now dribbling the ball, smirking.

"Give me the ball," Fiona said.

Lindy passed it to her, putting all her weight behind it. Fiona wouldn't allow herself to flinch as she caught it. She began dribbling again. "All right, girls, this is how you do a layup."

Fueled by anger and embarrassment, Fiona drove around Lindy, ignoring her out-stretched hands and banked the ball gently into the basket.

"The rest of you line up and see if you can do it." She walked over to Lindy. "Nice defense," she said.

Lindy shrugged.

"Since you know what you're doing, why don't you help your dad and demonstrate how to do a layup again. Okay?"

"All right. But I'm doing it for my dad, not you."

"Understood. Thanks, Lindy."

Fiona thought the girl muttered, "You're not welcome," as she ran toward her friends.

Fiona shook her head as she rubbed her elbow and watched the girls heave the ball at the hoop. Lindy might be having a hard time, but she was a little piece of work.

Thank goodness Fiona wasn't coaching her team.

CHAPTER ELEVEN

FIONA HELD the ice pack on her elbow and shifted in the easy chair that had once been her mother's in the living room. Her elbow was still throbbing, and it had been several hours since she'd fallen at practice.

Annabelle sat in front of the chair, flattening her ears as she watched Tasha in the chair next to her. Almost as soon as she'd sat down, Tasha had jumped into her lap. She'd been flattered by his attention.

Until she realized the cat didn't want to sit in her lap. He wanted the chair.

Now he was sprawled on his side next to her, taking up most of the space on the cushion. Fiona nudged him with her hip, but he was oblivious, apparently sound asleep.

"You are a load and a half."

He was probably faking it. "I was here first, buddy."

She tossed the book onto the floor. Okay,

she had officially become pathetic. She was having an argument with a cat over who got to sit in a chair.

"Maybe you need to think about who's dishing out your food," she said as she stood. Tasha stretched, easing himself into the center of the cushion, and Fiona smiled. "Slick move, dude."

The green curtain fluttered in a gust of cool air, and Fiona sighed with relief. It had been hot and humid all day. As if the cooler air had energized her, Annabelle barked and jumped at the chair Fiona had just deserted. Her front legs scrabbled at the cushion and she snarled at Tasha. The cat's tail twitched and he opened his eyes to stare at the dog. Annabelle lunged once more, then slid to the floor and landed on her side.

"Yeah, you're both tough. Real hard cases." Fiona scratched Annabelle's ears as the dog struggled to her feet. "Now go to your corners."

Annabelle tilted her head, then trotted away. "Good decision, Annie," Fiona said. "He'd take you with one paw tied behind his back."

Fiona's smile faded as she watched the dog turn and stumble. Annabelle caught herself before she could fall.

"What's wrong, baby? You've already had your insulin. It's not the diabetes, is it?" Fiona touched the dog's back, and Annabelle whipped her head around and snapped. Fiona snatched her hand away.

"Annabelle?" The dog staggered to the corner, where she collapsed in a heap. When Fiona crossed over and tentatively petted her, the dog thumped her tail weakly on the floor. She lay with her head on her front paws, watching Fiona.

The wind rushed past the window, fluttering the curtain, and rain poured down in a sudden torrent. Fiona flinched, then ran to close all the windows. By the time she got back to the living room, Annabelle was pacing the floor unsteadily.

Fiona crouched in front of her. "Is it the storm, Annie? Are you scared? Is that why you're acting so weird?" She picked the dog up and cradled her against her chest. "It's okay. I get scared during storms, too."

Annabelle was trembling. Or was that her own shivering? "I should take one of my pills," she said to the dog as the rain beat on the porch roof. "It sounds like it's going to be a bad storm."

She set the dog down to go upstairs, and

Annabelle flopped over like a rag doll. "Are you still sick?" The dog had vomited earlier after scarfing down part of a bag of spicy cheese chips Charlie had spilled.

Fiona pulled out her phone, then hesitated. She didn't want to call Jackson at home for a veterinary question. It felt somehow presumptuous.

She grabbed the phone book and looked up the number for Jackson's clinic. It was closed, but calling his answering service would give exactly the message she wanted. Impersonal. Professional.

After giving the woman who answered the phone the information about Annabelle and Fiona's phone number, she hung up and reached for the dog. But Annabelle didn't want to be held. She squirmed out of Fiona's hold to pace unsteadily around the room again.

Five minutes later the phone rang. "What's wrong, Fiona?" Jackson's voice.

She described Annabelle's symptoms and the earlier vomiting. "I'm not sure if she's sick or just scared of the storm. Should I bring her to the clinic?" She gripped the phone tightly as rain beat against the window. The wind whistled and rattled the window panes.

She didn't want to go out in this weather. Her

hands got clammy just thinking about it. And she couldn't take her Xanax if she had to drive.

"No. It would be faster if I came over to your house." He hesitated. "Is it okay if I bring the kids? I don't want to leave them alone. The electrical service in Spruce Lake goes out pretty regularly when it storms."

"Of course it's okay." She could hear them whining in the background, and Jackson spoke some sharp words to them. "Unless they would rather hang out with Charlie. He's at his father's house. I'm sure Ted wouldn't mind."

"I'll ask them." She could hear him speaking, but the words were muffled.

A moment later, he said, "Are you sure it's okay with Ted and Melody?"

"I'll call them, but they'd be thrilled if Charlie had friends over."

"Okay, thanks. I'll be there in ten minutes."

After calling Ted, Fiona held the unwilling Annabelle and paced from the living room to the kitchen and back again. Her elbow still throbbed. The storm was gathering in intensity. The sky had turned an ugly purple and the tree on the parkway bent almost in half in the wind. She shivered as she watched it.

"I need my pills," she murmured. Thunderstorms triggered anxiety attacks for her, and after years of trying unsuccessfully to cope, she'd finally agreed to take medication.

The doorbell rang before she'd taken three steps. When she opened the door, Jackson stepped inside, soaked in spite of his umbrella. "Nasty storm," he said as she shut the door fast. He set down the umbrella and a black bag and took off his wet jacket. He tossed it over the newel post and held out his arms for the dog. "Let me take a look at her."

"Thank you for coming here," Fiona said. "I didn't want to take her out in the rain if she's sick."

Liar. *She* was the one who didn't want to go out in the storm.

"Tell me what she was doing." He settled on the floor of the living room and began to examine Annabelle. Water glistened in Jackson's hair and slid down the back of his neck. Fiona reached out to wipe it away, then drew her hand away at the last moment.

She told him what had happened, starting with the cheese chip episode she'd mentioned on the phone. "I wondered if she was scared of the storm."

Jackson raised his eyebrows, but didn't say a thing. He palpated the dog's abdomen, looked in her mouth and her eyes, then set her on the floor to watch her walk. She was even more uncoordinated than she'd been earlier.

Rain lashed at the windows and Fiona glanced up. No lightning yet.

Jackson nodded at the ice pack she'd left on the floor. "What's the ice for? Did she feel hot to you?"

Fiona snatched it up and tossed it onto an end table. "No, that was for me."

"You're hurt?"

"Just precautionary."

"Lindy knocked you down at practice. What did she do to you?"

"Nothing, Jackson. I'm okay. Take care of my dog, not me."

He studied her for a long moment. "We're not finished talking about this," he said. "But we'll deal with Annabelle first. I'm going to need you to hold her so I can get a little blood sample." He put the dog in her arms and showed her how to hold a vein.

He used a tiny syringe to draw a few drops of blood from Annabelle's leg, then opened his bag and took out an instrument that looked vaguely like a calculator. He put a drop of blood on a little strip of paper, then stuck it into a slot on the side. A minute later he read a number, then set the machine aside.

"She's got low blood sugar. Did you give her an insulin shot this evening?"

"Of course I did." She hadn't missed one yet.

"Then it's probably because of the vomiting. If she was at the clinic, I'd put her on an IV with sugar in it. But I'd rather not start an IV here." He rummaged in the bag and pulled out a small bottle. "This is a concentrated sugar solution. I'll give her some of it orally."

She watched as Jackson drew the clear liquid into a second syringe, removed the needle, then lifted Annabelle's lip and began squirting the contents into the side of her mouth. The dog's tongue came out and she started to lick.

"That's my girl," Jackson crooned as he dribbled the solution into Annabelle's mouth until he'd given it all to her.

"Is she going to be okay?" Fiona asked anxiously.

Jackson smiled. "Good as new in a couple of minutes." He rummaged in his bag and pulled out a vial of white liquid and another syringe. By the time he'd filled it, Annabelle was walking normally and sniffing at the chair where Tasha sat. The cat was staring at the window. What was there to see? Nothing but wind and rain.

"Scratch her ears," Jackson ordered after he'd retrieved her. While she did, he injected the liquid into Annabelle's thigh.

"What was that for?" Fiona asked.

"For the vomiting. I'm guessing you'd just fed her and she tossed up most of her food. That's what made her blood sugar drop after you gave her the insulin."

Jackson petted the dog absently while he dropped the vial and used syringe into his bag.

Fiona flinched when thunder rumbled overhead. First time. There would be more. She reached for her purse, her hands beginning to shake. "How much do I owe you?"

Jackson snapped his bag shut. "Why didn't you call me yourself? Why did you use my answering service?"

Fiona dug in her purse for her wallet instead of looking at him. "It felt presumptuous to call you directly. I didn't want to make any assumptions."

"What kind of assumptions didn't you want to make, Fiona?" He set his bag on the hall table.

Silence stretched like a rubber band pulled tighter and tighter. A bolt of lightning lit up the living room. She tossed the purse onto the table. "We're not friends, Jackson. We don't have any kind of a relationship. Under the circumstances, I thought it best to keep it professional."

"What circumstances would that be?"

"I don't think I need to spell it out for you."

"Please do. I want to be clear."

"That little incident in the parking lot of the Lake House."

He tugged the sleeve of her T-shirt, rubbing the fabric between his fingers. "What about that 'little incident'? Have you been thinking about me?"

She yanked away from him. "Of course not. Frankly, I've been so busy I forgot about it until tonight."

He leaned against the end of the staircase like he was planning on being there awhile. "Yeah, me, too." He shifted so that he was leaning toward her. "Why did you have me take the kids over to Ted Cross's house tonight?"

"I could hear them when I called you. They sounded upset about coming over here."

His mouth twitched, and she bent to pet Annabelle at her feet.

"My dog was sick! I was worried! Do you think I was planning some kind of seduction scene?"

"A guy can always hope."

"Do you have a lot of clients who lure you to their houses with stories about sick dogs? Do they meet you in negligees? Or is that just a fantasy of yours?"

His eyes gleamed. "Never has been in the past."

Before she could respond, a huge crash of thunder shook the house. She recoiled and looked outside. Sheets of rain pounded on the window, and the wind howled.

"Do you want to stay here until the storm lets up?" she asked. "You'll get soaked if you try to leave now." And she'd be alone in the house.

He reached for his phone. "Let me make sure Logan and Lindy are okay at the Crosses'."

Fiona glanced up the stairs. She should go up there and get one of the damn Xanax. But maybe she'd be okay if Jackson stayed.

And she didn't want him to know about the stupid panic attacks.

His phone snapped shut and she turned around. Too late to get a pill. "Are the kids all right?"

"They're in no hurry to come home. Melody Cross is baking cookies, and they've already had popcorn and soda."

"Do you want something to drink? Beer?

Wine? Iced tea?" Maybe by the time he finished a drink, the storm would be over.

"Are you going to give me that look of yours if I ask for a beer?"

"What look is that?"

"That suspicious, are-you-just-like-your-old-man look."

It stung that he thought she'd be so judgmental. "You're nothing like your father. I know that."

"Just want to be clear." He stared at her. "You're pale. You okay?"

"Fine." She tried to control the shivering brought on by the almost constant lightning. "Let me see what's in the fridge."

She opened the refrigerator door but stared blindly inside, not seeing a thing. The wind rattled the old window in its frame, whistling into the kitchen.

"How about one of those beers?" Jackson said from behind her. He put a hand on her shoulder. "You want one, too?"

"No, thanks," she said, trying to keep her teeth from chattering. She'd been fooling herself that she could get by without the pills, and they didn't mix well with alcohol. She grabbed a longneck Leinenkugel, but it almost slipped out of her hand.

"Got it," Jackson said, catching the beer. "Slippery devil with this humidity."

"Yeah." She leaned against the refrigerator door, hiding her trembling hands behind her back. "You want a glass?"

"Nah. Glasses are for girly men."

"Check. Jackson. Manly man." Her teeth had started to chatter, and she clamped her mouth shut. She slid around him and backed out of the kitchen. The pills were in her bedroom. At the top of the stairs and around the corner. Thirty steps, max. Maybe forty.

"Are you all right, Fee?" He frowned as he followed her. "You're white as a sheet and sweating."

"It's hot in here with all the windows closed. Aren't you hot?"

"I was." He studied her carefully. "Now I'm a little worried."

"I'm fine." She groped for the banister behind her, finally connecting with the cool wood. "I need something from upstairs. I'll be right back, okay?"

Something thumped on the roof of the house, and she jumped. "What was that?"

"Sounded like a tree branch." He opened the front door and peered into the storm as she backed away. "It's blowing hard out here.

Didn't sound big enough to do any damage, though. I wouldn't worry about it."

Easy for him to say. She struggled to breathe through the tiny pinhole her windpipe had become. She turned and grabbed the wood railing. She remembered what storms sounded like on the second floor of this house. The ceilings weren't insulated and the rain on the roof sounded like boulders crashing down a mountain.

She'd only taken one step when Jackson put his arm in front of her. "Hold it."

"What?"

"Listen."

She forced herself to concentrate. Over the din of the rain and wind, she heard the Spruce Lake tornado siren wailing.

CHAPTER TWELVE

"WE NEED TO GO to the basement," Jackson said. He yanked open the door and tugged her toward it. "Go on down and I'll grab the animals."

"Charlie's snakes," she managed to say. "I have to get them, too."

Jackson's hand tightened on her arm. "I'll do it. Where are they?"

"Upstairs. Zoe's old room."

"Take Tasha and Annabelle downstairs. I'll find the snakes." Without waiting for her to answer, he ran up the stairs. As the siren wailed, she heard him moving around in Charlie's room, swearing.

Tasha was still on the chair in the living room, and Annabelle was lying in her bed next to the chair. The storm didn't seem to bother them at all.

Her head spinning, Fiona shuddered at the yawning blackness of the basement and groped for the switch at the top landing. The bulb over the stairs cast shadows on the walls and railing. Everything past the last step remained dark.

They hadn't cleaned out the basement yet. It was full of dusty old lawn furniture, luggage and boxes that had been stored years ago. But she'd be safer down there with the dust and the cobwebs. And the memories.

She wanted to curl into a ball and shut out everything—the smell of ozone from the lightning, the rush of the wind, the shriek of the siren. "Annabelle," she called, unable to move, and the dog's ears perked up. "Come on, baby. We need to go downstairs."

Annabelle opened her eyes. The wind screamed, and hail pelted the house with thousands of tiny, sharp thuds against the siding.

It felt as if Fiona's feet were nailed to the floor. "Annabelle," she pleaded. "Come here. Please. Tasha." Her voice sharpened. "Come here, boy."

They both gave her a bored look. She forced herself to take one step, then another.

She heard Jackson on the stairs behind her, grunting with the effort of carrying the snakes' terrariums. "Fiona. Why are you still up here?"

"Getting the animals," she said. "Be right down."

He headed into the basement, and the siren shrilled louder, until she could hear nothing else. She clapped her hands over her ears and stumbled forward. When she finally reached the chair, she tucked Annabelle, bed and all, under one arm, then grabbed Tasha with the other. She was two feet from the door when Jackson reappeared.

"What's taking so long?" he asked. He took Annabelle out of her arms. "Come on, Fee. The siren is still blowing."

She followed him to the doorway, took a deep breath and clutched the railing. Tasha struggled, his rear nails digging into her, and she held him more tightly. She was halfway down when Jackson appeared out of the darkness below her and took the cat.

He pulled the door closed, then wrapped an arm around her and hurried her the rest of the way.

He let her go when they reached the bottom of the stairs. "Where's the light switch?"

"The wall on your left," she gasped. "Have to go upstairs. Need something."

"Are you nuts?" He turned on the lights. "There's a tornado somewhere close."

"Have to." Hands shaking, she grabbed the railing and pulled herself up. Toward the storm.

"No jewelry is worth risking your life," he said, catching her around the waist and carrying her back. "Settle down, Fee."

"I…can't." Air whistled in and out as she struggled to breathe. "Let…me go. Now."

Annabelle barked, a sharp, short noise, and Tasha rubbed against her leg. Jackson's hands gentled on her shoulders. "Fiona. What's wrong? And don't tell me nothing, damn it."

She wrapped her arms around herself. She hadn't faced a storm without her Xanax in years. And never in this house.

"Pills," she wheezed. "Need them. Now."

He bent to look more closely at her. "What kind of…oh my God." He wrapped his arms around her and held her tightly. "You're having a panic attack," he said. "Because of the storm."

She nodded against his chest.

"You have Valium or Xanax or something like that. Upstairs?"

She nodded again. If he let her go, she could find them.

She didn't want him to let her go.

The realization filtered through her racing heart, her tight chest, that she needed Jackson.

She didn't want to need him. Didn't want to feel so comforted by his presence.

But she couldn't make herself let him go.

He turned off all but one set of lights and drew her into a corner. He held her close with one arm as he fumbled with one of the old lawn chairs. She kept her head buried in his shoulder and her arms around him.

"We're going to sit down, Fee," he said. He picked her up as if she weighed nothing, then eased her onto his lap. "We're going to stretch out, okay?"

He waited until she nodded, then slid her next to him on the old chaise longue. As she curled into a ball, she recognized the stiff, yellowing cushion. She and her sisters had spent hours on it during the summer, reading beneath the shade of the maple tree in the yard. Dust rose when she shifted, and she sneezed.

"Okay, Fee. We're in the corner of the basement. The snakes are down here, Annabelle is in her bed and Tasha is on top of a workbench on the other side of the room. We're all safe. I know you need your pills, but we can't get them. I'll help you through this." He rubbed her back in a slow, circular pattern and maneuvered her head beneath his chin.

"Your hair still smells like grapefruit," he

murmured as he threaded his fingers through it. "I was probably the only guy at the college who got turned-on when he ate breakfast."

His other hand continued its soothing circles, and the tightness in her lungs began to ease. He smelled like fabric softener and coffee and Jackson. Her heart boomed against her chest, but the erratic rhythm was slowing and evening out. The siren blared, but the sound of the storm was muted by the steady beat of Jackson's heart.

The chill in the basement cooled her sweat-slick skin, and she shivered. He shifted so he was facing her. "Are you cold? Do you need a blanket?"

"Don't leave."

"I'm not going anywhere. I can reach it from here."

He leaned across her, pushing his body more firmly against hers. Then he pulled a blanket over her. She sneezed again.

"The storm will be over soon," he said, tucking her closer beneath the blanket. "In the meantime, you're safe. I'm here, and I'm not going anywhere."

Soon. Soon wasn't too long. She could do soon. Rain battered against the narrow basement windows, and she held Jackson more tightly. As she shifted to get her ear closer to Jackson's heart, to let the steady beat calm her, she felt the hard length of his erection against her stomach. She froze.

"It's okay, Fee. I'm not going to jump your bones. Automatic reaction. I could probably get a grant to study it. Might find a lot of men don't need those blue pills. Just give them a sniff of grapefruit."

His arms tightened. "Or maybe it's you, and the grapefruit is secondary. Now that's a study I'd get behind. Or maybe in front of. Which do you think?"

A vise gripped her chest and her body shuddered so hard that her muscles ached, but she smiled against his chest. She burrowed closer.

"Pretty sneaky way of getting out of discussing why you need that ice pack," he said. Something touched her hair. His mouth? "You could have just told me it's none of my business. I wouldn't have paid any attention, but you could have tried. Then you'd get all bossy and snooty. I like you snooty. Icy and cold like a Popsicle. Makes me want to—"

"J-Jackson. Stop it." A different kind of tremor shook her.

"Are you getting bossy? Oh, yeah." His

hand on her back dipped a little lower and brushed the top of her hips, lighting a fire inside her. "Bring it. Give it your best shot."

She knew what he was doing. He was trying to distract her. He was trying to make her laugh. That was all. But she gripped him more tightly and moved so that she cradled him with her hips. So that he was pressed against the most sensitive part of her.

She lifted her head and kissed him, clinging to his lips. His hips rocked against hers and he kissed her back. She put his hand on her breast, and he swept his thumb across her nipple. She forgot about the storm raging outside.

Then Jackson eased away from her. "Sorry, Fee," he said. "Not going to happen. God knows I want you." He pressed his hips against hers, and she couldn't hide her response. "I think you want me, too. But I'm not going to be a substitute tranquilizer." He turned onto his side. "How about a rain check? Cobwebs and dusty lounge chairs aren't quite the ambience I had in mind. I want you in a bed, and hours to play with you."

A bed. She wanted that, too. And it would be such a huge mistake.

"Sorry," she said, releasing him.

He wrapped his arms more tightly around

her. "You're not going anywhere. I guess we need a different distraction. How about a fight? I can do a fight."

"I like fighting," she said.

He gripped her harder, then he smoothed his palm down her arm. "Can you believe this? I've lost my mind." With his other hand, he continued to caress her back. Thunder rumbled, but it was in the distance now. And the siren had stopped. "The hottest woman on the planet is making major moves on me and I'm saying no. Better call the coroner, because I'm dead. Only explanation."

His tone was teasing, but he was hard as steel when she curled into him. "Thank you, Jackson," she said. Her chest still felt tight, but she could breathe. And her heart had slowed. The panic attack was over. She cupped his face in her hands. "I don't know what I would have done without you."

He sat up and turned her face toward one of the lights. "You okay? You don't look okay yet."

"I'm shaky and thirsty and tired. But the panic is gone. You got me through it."

"You got yourself through it. I just held you and distracted you while you did it." He shifted her off his lap. "We have to stay down here until they blow the all-clear signal. Usually takes about fifteen minutes."

"Okay." Rain still hit the basement windows, but the fury was gone. Had she actually just tried to get Jackson to make love with her in this dirty, depressing basement? In the middle of a storm?

It must have been some odd reaction to the panic attack. Something to do with the adrenaline.

"I'm going to call Logan and Lindy and make sure everyone is okay over there," he said. He pulled his phone out and punched in a number. There was silence for a long moment.

"Everybody's probably trying to make calls," he said, disconnecting, but his hand tightened on the phone. "I'll try again in a minute." He ran his fingers over her hair and down her back. "Is there any water in the basement?"

"Bree put a case of bottled water down here earlier in the summer when Charlie started running. There might be some left."

She stood to look for it and stumbled on her still-shaky legs. Jackson eased her onto the chaise longue. "Stay here. I'll find it."

The dim light from his phone glowed suddenly, and she saw him punch a button. She heard the fast busy signal, and he closed the phone. Moments later he was back with two bottles. He opened one and handed it to her, then drank the other down in a few gulps. Setting the empty bottle on the stairs, he sat next to her again and looped an arm around her shoulders.

"Do you want to talk about it?"

"About what? The panic attacks?"

"Do you have them often?"

"Only when it storms." She sighed and picked at the label on the bottle. "The first time it happened, I freaked out. Thought I was having a heart attack. Dying. The doctor I saw sent me to a therapist. It didn't take long for us to figure it out."

"Yeah?" He brushed his hand up and down her arm, soothing and reassuring. She didn't talk about the panic attacks with anyone. Not even her sisters. It felt like a weakness. A flaw. Like she couldn't control herself.

But she wanted to tell Jackson.

"My mother died in a storm. She'd gone out to get my father more pipe tobacco, and her car skidded on the wet pavement. She hit a light pole and it fell onto the car and killed her." She stared at her lap and realized her fists were clenched.

"My mom loved my jewelry. She always encouraged me. She wore my first pieces—these stupid earrings I made by heating up marbles then throwing them in cold water. They got all cracked inside and I thought they were so cool."

Her throat swelled and she took a deep breath. "They were really ugly, but she wore them anyway. She said they'd be worth a fortune when I was a famous jewelry designer."

She stood again and walked over to the cobweb-festooned window. Raindrops slid down the glass. "My mom assumed I'd make it as a jewelry designer. She told me I was brilliant and creative and had a gift."

Her breath fogged the window, and she drew a tiny heart on it. "After she died, my dad would get angry when I spent time working on my designs. He told me I'd better figure out a way to make a living, because no one was going to pay good money for pieces of metal and stones. Every time it rained, it was a reminder that my mother had died getting my father's tobacco. I hated the bastard. The panic attacks started after Mom died."

He came up behind her and wrapped his

arms around her. "I'm so sorry, Fee." He kissed her neck, and she shivered. "You always handle it by yourself, don't you?"

There wasn't anyone to help her handle it. "If I'm lucky, they happen in my apartment."

"If it storms again while you're here, I'll come over. I liked distracting you."

"Yeah, I could tell."

He traced her spine with his fingers, and she shivered again. "I think you liked it, too."

Too much. She stared blindly at the rain leaving wet trails down the window. "Try the kids again," she said. "I want to make sure they're okay."

He punched a number on his phone, and this time after only a couple of rings, someone answered. Jackson tilted the phone toward her so she could hear, too.

"Dad?" Lindy's voice. "Where are you?"

"I'm still with Fiona. The siren went off before I could leave. Are you and Logan and Charlie all right? Mr. and Mrs. Cross?"

"We're fine," Lindy said. She paused. "I wish you were here. I was scared."

"She was not." Logan's voice, louder than Lindy's. "Charlie's dad has an awesome TV in the basement. We're watching *Pirates of the Caribbean* and we could barely hear the siren."

"I'll be there as soon as I can," Jackson said. "Behave yourself, Lind."

"I am." Even from a distance, there was no mistaking the sulky tone of Lindy's voice.

"I love you, sweet pea. Logan, too."

Fiona moved away as Jackson shut the phone and slid it back into his pocket. "I'm sorry you were stuck here instead of with your kids. You must have been frantic."

"I was terrified. I wanted to be there. Protecting them. But I couldn't. Racing over there during a tornado would have been plain stupid."

Fiona snuck a look at her watch. Less than ten minutes had passed. Now that the panic had eased, she wanted Jackson to leave. Her nerves felt raw, as if they were exposed to the air. She hated feeling so vulnerable.

"You're getting all weird about what happened, aren't you?" Jackson said from behind her.

"Don't be ridiculous. I make a fool of myself in front of men every day."

He turned her around and lifted her chin so she was looking at him. "You weren't a fool. You were in the middle of a panic attack and you thought of the animals. Even those snakes of Charlie's. That's amazing, Fee."

He wrapped her in his arms again and pulled her close. "You're incredible."

She allowed herself to relax against him for a moment. He felt so good—solid and strong, familiar. As if he could protect her from anything.

She eased away. "It's probably safe to go upstairs."

"Yeah." He didn't move, though. "You're going to make yourself nuts over this, aren't you?"

Yes, she was. "What are you talking about?"

Before he could answer, the wind died completely, replaced by an eerie silence. Then, all of a sudden, the tornado siren blared again.

The wind screamed outside the window. It sounded as if a train was bearing down on them.

Jackson hauled her into the corner of the basement just as a huge crash shook the house.

CHAPTER THIRTEEN

THE BASEMENT LIGHTS went out, plunging them into darkness. Annabelle whined, and Tasha let out an unearthly howl. Fiona grabbed Jackson. The siding on the house groaned, and she heard glass break. Something big hit the floor directly above them, and she flinched.

"You're okay, Fee. You're safe down here," he said, easing her to sit on the floor with him. "You going to have another panic attack?" Her back was to the wall and Jackson covered the rest of her.

"I hope not." She twisted her fists in his shirt and held on tightly. "Maybe. Keep talking."

"You think the movie's still going—the kids are still in the basement at Ted's?"

"Ted is Mr. Responsible," she told him, easing away from his chest to look at him. "He'll make sure they're safe."

"I shouldn't have dropped them off at his house. I should have kept them with me."

"You didn't know this would happen." She leaned back so she could see him better. "You heard Logan. They're having a party. They're fine, Jackson." *God, make sure they are safe.*

He blew out a long breath, then untangled her hand from his shirt and kissed her palm. "I'm supposed to distract you, not the other way around."

"Yeah, you're falling down on the job, Grant." She ignored her fears. It wasn't about her this time. "Have you seen Ted's house? It's huge. Brick. Not a flimsy wooden place like this. And we're okay. The kids probably can't even hear the storm."

He fumbled his phone open and pushed a button. Busy.

He pulled her to her feet. The wind had died down yet again. "What's going on up there?" she asked.

"Hard to tell," he said, and he slipped the phone into his pocket. "But I think a tornado just went by."

"A tornado?" Her hands tightened on his shirt. "Really?"

"It sure sounded like one."

The siren rose and fell. Then it stopped abruptly. Rain still beat on the windows, but there was no thunder. No flashes of lightning. Nothing but the creaking of the house.

"Is it gone?"

"Probably. But we're not going anywhere."

Annabelle was plastered to her leg, and Fiona uncurled one hand from Jackson's shirt to pet her. Tasha stood at the bottom of the stairs, staring up.

Jackson pulled his phone out again and punched the button. "Circuits are probably still busy," he muttered.

"Hey, Dad. Are you okay?" Logan's voice.

"We're fine. What about you guys?" Jackson said. Fiona put her head next to his so she could hear.

"No worries." He cleared his throat. "It's dark, but it'll be easier to scare Lindy now." Even though his voice was tinny and far away, Fiona heard the fear beneath the boy's bravado.

"We're going to stay put until we get the all clear. Let me talk to Lindy.

"Hey, baby," he said a moment later. "How are you holding up?"

"I'm scared, Daddy." Her voice skipped on a sob.

"I know, honey. I was, too. But the siren stopped and we'll be out of here before you know it. Then I'll come over and get you."

"We'll be waiting for you, Daddy." The fear in her voice reminded Fiona that Lindy was still a child.

"Is Charlie there?"

He handed Fiona the phone, warm from his hand. In a moment, Charlie said, "Hey, Aunt Fee. You okay?"

"I'm fine. How are you doing?"

"It's boring, now that we can't watch TV anymore. Ted and Melody kind of freaked out. Good thing we were here." More preteen boy bravado.

Fiona choked back a laugh. "I'm sure they appreciate you taking care of them."

"Yeah."

"We brought the snakes down in the basement."

"Thanks, Aunt Fee."

"I'll come get you soon. In the meantime, let me talk to Ted…or Melody."

"I'll see you whenever."

After reassuring Ted that she and Jackson would be over for the kids as soon as they could, Fiona shut the phone and gave it back to Jackson. "Were you that macho when you were twelve?"

"Probably worse. I had a lot more to prove than Logan or Charlie. I think it's safe to come out of the corner." He brushed at her hair and back. "Cobwebs."

"What did you have to prove?" she asked, brushing at her chest and legs.

His hands stilled on her, then he let her go. "You know what my father was. The town drunk. The guy everyone laughed at. That put me at the bottom of the teenage pecking order. I had to prove I was tougher than anyone."

"Not to me, you didn't."

"Never to you." His voice softened. "You didn't care who my old man was." He skimmed his hand over her hair, lingered at her neck. "You were a miracle, Fee. Until you dumped me and took off."

The basement was pitch-black. The small rectangles of window were only marginally lighter. She could barely see Jackson, but every molecule of her body felt him. She wanted to tell him she was sorry she'd hurt him.

"I found the chaise longue we were sitting on before," he said, his tone cooler. More distant.

As she followed his voice and sat next to him, he said, "I don't suppose you have any flashlights down here?"

"Probably, but I have no idea where they'd be."

"I hope you're not afraid of the dark."

"I'm a big girl, Jackson."

"Already figured that out," he said. He leaned closer.

Then something tickled her foot, and she barely managed to swallow a shriek as she yanked her feet up to the cushion, frantically brushing them off. She'd only been down here a few times since she got home, and once she'd seen a bug at least a couple of inches long with hundreds of legs. She hugged her knees to her chest.

"Bug. On my foot." She shuddered.

"Saved by the bug, Fee?"

The scent of arousal filled the darkness between them. His? Hers? "Do you think I wanted to be saved?"

"I don't know what you want."

She touched his face, felt the rough rasp of his beard, the mouth she could never resist, the angle of his chin. "My home is New York, Jackson." She pulled back her hand. "I've built too much to just leave it all behind." Even if, just for a little while, she wanted to forget everything but him.

"So it's just *me* you find it easy to leave behind, then?" He caught her face between his hands and kissed her, his mouth hard, his fingers tangling in her hair. Startled, her body betrayed her and she turned into him, his body against hers. Hers aching for him.

As they tumbled back onto the chaise longue, they landed on Tasha. He yowled, then scrambled away.

Jackson lay still for a moment, then pulled her upright. He stood. "I'm going to see what it looks like upstairs."

She should probably follow him. It was her dad's house, after all. "Annabelle?" she said softly. "Want to sit up here with me?"

Annabelle jumped onto the chair and Fiona hugged her. The end of the chaise longue moved, and she realized that Tasha had returned.

"It's okay, Tasha," she said, stroking him.

Jackson clattered down the stairs. "I couldn't get the door open. Something's blocking it."

Visions of the house destroyed played in her mind. What about her studio? Was it intact? Her entire stock of metal and stones was in that garage. And she didn't have the money to replace them. "What do you think it is? What happened?"

"Don't panic, Fee." He rubbed her arm. "We'll call the police and they'll get us out."

"Don't tell me not to panic. Something's wrong." She jerked her arm away. "Could you see anything?"

"A window's open. I could feel the breeze beneath the door. That's all."

She hadn't left any windows open. "I need to get out of here."

Jackson pulled out his phone and dialed 911.

SUNLIGHT STREAMED weakly through the narrow basement windows as Jackson tried to roll over on the narrow chaise longue. His hip bumped into the armrest, and he muttered an oath. He put out his hand and found Fiona. Soft, warm and sound asleep.

Even half-asleep, he knew who it was. Tucking his arm around her waist, he pulled her against him.

It had taken an hour to get through to the police. The harried desk clerk had asked if anyone was injured, then told him officers would get there as fast as they could. He'd called Logan and Lindy and explained the situation, and Ted had assured him they had plenty of room.

He and Fiona had lain side by side in the darkness. Barely speaking.

His arm had fallen asleep.

She was the one who got away. She was always going to be larger than life, the idealized woman no one else could compete with. Including Mallory.

Of course he still wanted Fiona. And tonight, it had felt as if she wanted him, too. Damn it. He wasn't about to pack his kids up and start his practice all over again in Manhattan. Even if he did, he doubted Fiona would want him to. He was utterly drained.

Someone pounded on the door at the top of the stairs. "You okay down there?"

Jackson eased off the chaise longue and hurried up to the door. "Can you get this open?"

"Jackson?" It was Jamie Evans.

"Yeah. Fiona McInnes is down here, too. Why can't we get it open?"

"A table fell over. Heavy-ass thing." He could hear Jamie grunting, then the door swung open. Sunlight made Jackson squint.

"You both all right?"

"We're fine." He rolled his shoulders and looked around. A window had blown out in the living room, and pieces of glass glittered on the carpet. The couch in front of the window was soaking wet and covered with glass, as well.

"We heard a crash. Thank God that's all it was."

"Not quite," Jamie said. He nodded toward the kitchen.

Annabelle trotted up the stairs, and Jackson picked her up with one hand. He turned the corner and stopped.

"Damn."

"Yeah," Jamie said.

A tree now filled the kitchen. The floor was soaking wet, and water glistened on the leaves. Holding on to the dog, he stepped into the room and looked around.

Part of the roof and back wall of the kitchen was missing. Sunlight poured in through the opening. The tree trunk had knocked over the refrigerator and crushed the counter. Several cabinets had been partly torn out of the wall and hung at crazy angles. Broken china littered the floor. The table was knocked on its side and the chairs were beneath the tree.

"Oh my God," Fiona said from behind him, staring at the devastation, gripping the cat. "Bree and Parker were going to live here."

"No one's living here for a while," Jamie said. "But I took a look outside, and it's not as bad as it looks."

"Not as bad as it looks?" She transferred her gaze to Jamie. "It looks pretty damn bad."

"The car in the driveway is totaled—"

"What?"

"—but insurance should cover that."

She moved to step into the kitchen, but Jackson held her back. "There's a lot of broken glass. Leave it for now."

She turned around and headed out the front. Jackson trailed behind her with the dog. He didn't want Annabelle to cut her feet on the glass.

The huge tree that used to stand in the backyard next door had split down the middle like a banana peel. One half had fallen on the fence and her new garden. The other half had crushed Fiona's car and devastated the kitchen.

The car roof was now level with the trunk. Both front tires were flat and the engine compartment was deeply dented.

"Bree's car is wrecked," she whispered. "What if I'd been in it when the tree fell? What if Charlie had been?"

He wanted to hold her, but her arms were full of struggling cat. "You're clutching him too tight. Don't let him go, though," he warned as she started to set the cat down. "There's too much that can hurt him."

"I have to call Zoe," she said. "I have to see how she is."

"Here's my cell." He exchanged it for the cat, juggling both pets.

After the dog relieved herself on the lawn, Jackson put both animals into his undamaged truck. He'd take them into the clinic for now. Assuming he still had a clinic.

One thing at a time.

Broken branches littered the street. An electric line was down at the end of the block, and the regional electric company already had trucks out. No other houses showed major damage, but the McInnes house couldn't be the only one hit.

How many people were injured? How many pets?

He needed to get Logan and Lindy. He needed to check his house and the clinic. It was going to be a busy day.

CHAPTER FOURTEEN

WHEN JACKSON RETURNED from putting the animals in his truck, Fiona was missing. "Where did she go?" he asked Jamie.

The police officer jerked his head toward the garage that was her studio. "In there. I told her to wait, but she didn't pay any attention."

"Really? I'm shocked. She's normally so docile." He started toward the studio, but Jamie grabbed his arm.

"Where are you going?"

"Where do you think, Evans?"

Jamie let him go, shaking his head. "It's sad to see a strong man become putty in the hands of a woman."

Jackson paused to glare over his shoulder. "You should know, cop boy. Is it true that you say 'yes, ma'am' on the way up when Helen tells you to jump?"

Jamie grinned. "Dude, anything that woman wants, she gets."

His friend's happiness sent a sliver of envy into Jackson. Ignoring it, he hurried toward the garage. "That's pathetic, Evans."

"You *wish* you were so pathetic!" Jamie called.

Not true. No woman was going to have the power to hurt him again.

He remembered Fiona in the darkness, arching into him, holding on to him.

He was in control now. He was going to stay far away from her.

As soon as he got her out of this falling-down garage.

Ragged curls of peeling paint on the door revealed the damp, gray wood beneath. Shabby and neglected, just like the house, and the storm had only made it worse. About half of the shingles were missing and the building listed to the side. He thought he heard it creak in the breeze.

He was surprised the storm hadn't knocked it down. It looked as if old man McInnes hadn't done any upkeep for years. Probably too busy being important at the college.

Even after almost thirteen years, the memory of Fiona's father still left a bitter taste in Jackson's mouth. If he hadn't been such a snob, would Fiona have been more open about their relationship? More flexible?

Would it have changed anything?

No way to know. And it wasn't important. He couldn't change the past, and neither could Fiona.

It didn't make a damn bit of difference now.

He pushed into the room without knocking. Fiona was kneeling in front of her safe. The door was open and one of the shelves was pulled out.

"What the hell are you doing in here?" he demanded.

She glanced up at him, then turned back to the safe. "Making sure everything is still here," she said. She pushed in that drawer, pulled out another one, then finally closed it and shut the safe. She spun the combination wheel and stood. "What's wrong, Jackson?"

"This building looks like it's going to collapse any minute," he said, resisting the impulse to drag her out by force. "You shouldn't be in here."

"Help me move the centrifuge, then," she said, gripping one side of the machine. "I need to get it someplace safe."

"Leave the damn centrifuge, Fiona! This is crazy."

She straightened. "Jackson, I need this centrifuge if I'm going to keep making jewelry. I have a lot of work to do before my show. If I can't keep working, my career is over. Either help me or get the hell out of my way."

She lifted the machine and staggered toward the door. Cursing, he took the other end and they carried it outside.

"Leave it here while I get the rest of my stuff," she said. "I need my tools. I think the safe is all right where it is for now. Even if the garage comes down, the safe will survive."

He followed her back in. While she picked up boxes of gems off the floor, she said, "If you're going to yell at me, leave now. If you want to help, I need the tools on the table and the floor in there." She pointed at a red metal toolbox against the wall. Then she grabbed her acetylene torch and soldering iron and carried them outside. By the time he'd finished packing all the delicate instruments, she'd removed almost everything else.

"The kids are waiting for us," he said.

She rounded on him. "If you want to get them, go ahead. I can take care of this stuff myself."

"How are you going to carry the centrifuge?" he asked.

"I'll manage."

"Just like you manage everything else, right? You're so damn single-minded about your work. It drives me crazy."

"I guess it's a good thing I moved far away so my career didn't upset you, then. And here I thought you'd never understand why I had to leave you behind," she said quietly.

She stared at him for a long moment, then she turned away and bent to pick up the centrifuge.

He bit off an oath and stooped to get the other end. They maneuvered carefully through the fallen tree, then put the machine in the hallway of the house. After a couple more trips, all her equipment was protected.

"Anything else to do before we get our children?" he asked.

"Nothing at all," she said coolly. "Let's go."

Neither of them spoke as they drove toward Ted's house. Several of the houses on Fiona's street had pieces of their roofs ripped off and there was another car crushed by a fallen tree. As they got farther away, there were a lot of downed branches but no other serious damage.

"Looks like your street got the worst of it," he finally said.

"I hope no one was hurt." She was staring out the window, her face hidden.

The silence was full of unspoken words. "Where are you and Charlie going to stay?"

She shrugged. "Zoe and Gideon's, probably."

"You can stay with us, if you'd like."

"Thank you, Jackson. I appreciate the offer, but we'll be fine."

"Zoe and Gideon live in a two-bedroom house. What are you going to do? Camp in the backyard?"

She leaned against the upholstery and closed her eyes. "Not your problem."

"Even after last night?"

"You were great last night," she said without looking at him. "I appreciate your help."

"Fiona, we almost had sex on that chair thing in your basement. Why are you acting like a stranger?"

Finally she shifted in the seat so she faced him. "I thought we connected last night. I thought we…shared a lot. But if you don't get it why my work is so important to me, frankly, I don't have the energy to explain it. I have a nephew to take care of and a business to rescue."

The truck rolled to a stop at the curb

outside Ted Cross's house. Small branches littered the lawns on the street, but there was no major damage. Was Jackson's house all right? A torrent of guilt rushed her.

He started to get out of the truck, and she touched his arm. "Jackson?"

"Yeah?" One foot out the door, he turned to her.

"I'm sorry I made you move my stuff. We should have gotten the kids and checked your house first. That was…that was selfish of me."

"It's okay, Fee," he said. "Nothing was going to change in the fifteen minutes it took to get your equipment put away." He slid out, then came around and opened her door for her. "Let's see how the kids are doing."

She got out and stepped away from him. "The kids might be watching."

"So what?"

"I wouldn't want them to get the wrong idea."

He stopped. "What idea would that be?"

"That there's something going on between us."

"There isn't, is there?"

"Of course not," she said hastily. "But Lindy might think so."

"I'll have a talk with her." He craned his head to look at her elbow. "She gave you a bruise."

"Don't say anything. What happens at practice stays at practice. Okay?"

"Why are you standing up for my kid?" he asked. "She hasn't even been nice to you."

"Drop it, Jackson." She pressed the doorbell.

Moments later the door opened and Lindy threw herself into Jackson's arms.

"Where were you, Daddy?"

Guilt made Fiona look away. She'd been selfish and stubborn.

"A table fell over in Fiona's house and blocked the door. We had to wait for the police to come and let us out." Jackson hugged her.

"You should have been with us." She glowered at Fiona, then called into the house, "Charlie. Your aunt is here." Lindy made her title sound like a dirty word.

A few minutes later they were out the door with all three kids after explaining to Ted and Melody that Jackson hadn't seen his house yet. As they headed for the truck, Lindy stopped on the sidewalk. "Where's your car?" she asked Fiona.

"Beneath a tree. I have to call a rental company and get one until my sister's can be fixed up. If that's even possible."

"So you're coming to our house?" she asked, narrowing her eyes.

"We're going to check and make sure it's okay," Jackson said. "Then we're going to figure out where Fiona and Charlie are going to live. There's a lot of damage to the McInnes house."

"They're not going to stay with us."

Fiona closed her eyes. "No, Lindy. We're not."

"If they need to," Jackson said at the same time.

"They have other people they can stay with," Lindy said.

"Hey, thanks a lot, Lindy," Charlie grumbled. "I love you, too. *Not*."

The five-minute ride to Jackson's clinic seemed like an eternity in the ensuing silence. Annabelle, sitting in Fiona's lap, whined and licked her hand. Fiona wished she could whine, too, but contented herself with petting her dog. When they finally arrived, it was evident the clinic wasn't visibly damaged.

"I need to check on the animals," Jackson said. "We'll only be a minute. Fiona, bring Annabelle. Charlie, give me Tasha. We'll leave them here for now."

Fiona climbed out of the car and took a deep breath. Once they stepped inside, Jackson said, "Lindy was out of line. I'd like to believe it's because she was worried. You're welcome to stay with us."

"Thank you," she said. "But we can stay with Zoe. Or maybe at Parker's house. It would be easier."

"Probably," he acknowledged.

He led the way into the back and showed her where to put her animals. Then, after checking all the boarders and examining the clinic, they returned to his truck.

"The clinic's fine," he said to the kids. "Let's see how our house did. Maxine and Kinky need to go out, too."

His home was undamaged, other than a missing piece of fence. A garbage can lying in the yard must have knocked it down. The dogs were frantic to get out, and Fiona smiled as they raced around the yard with the kids.

"At least I can help you move your stuff," Jackson said as he leaned against the garage. His eyes followed Lindy around the yard.

They stopped at Parker's house, which wasn't damaged. When they returned to her father's, it didn't take long for her and Charlie to pack their belongings. As they carried their bags downstairs, Fiona saw Lindy examining the centrifuge on the floor of the hall.

"I use that to make jewelry," Fiona said.

Lindy pulled her hands away.

"It's all right. You won't hurt it."

Lindy glanced at her, then touched one of the tiny baskets. "This place is wrecked," she said gruffly. "It's okay if you stay with us."

"Thank you, Lindy." Fiona glanced outside. Had Jackson said something to her? "That's very nice of you to offer. But we're going to stay at Parker's house."

"Okay." She set one of the baskets on the centrifuge rocking.

"That's a centrifuge," Fiona said, watching her. "I use it to fill a mold with liquid metal."

"How does it work?"

Fiona shifted a box in her arms. "I'll tell you what. When I get it set up, I'll demonstrate it for you. Okay?"

Lindy glanced at her suspiciously, then touched the basket again. "I guess."

"We'll make something for you," Fiona said.

"Really?" Lindy's eyes lit up, then she shrugged. "I mean, I guess that might be interesting."

Fiona smiled as she carried the box out of the house.

"You look pretty happy for someone who's moving her stuff out of her wrecked house," Jackson said as he took the box and slid it into the back of the truck.

"I think Lindy and I just had a moment."

"A moment when you were tempted to kill her?"

"No. A nice one."

"Don't let it go to your head. It won't last."

Maybe not. But she'd take her moments where she could get them.

CHAPTER FIFTEEN

"For God's sake, Fee, cut yourself some slack." Zoe stood on the driveway, her hands on her hips. "You've been working on that tree all morning."

"I should have been out here yesterday," Fiona retorted. But her arms were trembling from the exertion of wielding the heavy chain saw. She carefully set it on the ground. "The tree people can't be here for a week, and we need to get the hole in the house covered."

"You shouldn't have to deal with this mess," Zoe said. "You should be fixing up a studio for yourself so you can get back to work."

She should be going back to New York. "Who's supposed to deal with this mess? You?"

"Absolutely." Zoe reached for the powerful tool. "I know how to use a chain saw."

Fiona stepped between her sister and the idling saw. "You think I'm going to let the mother of my unborn nieces or nephews swing a chain saw? Does it say stupid on my forehead?"

Zoe scowled. "You're as bad as Gideon."

"Yeah, I love you, too."

Zoe eased herself onto the steps of the porch with a sigh, absently rubbing her gently rounded abdomen. "It doesn't seem fair," she said quietly. "You hate this house, and you're the one who has to take care of it."

"Good thing I'm a fan of irony."

Zoe snorted as she leaned back against the railing. Fiona's arms ached as she picked up the saw. It roared to life and blue smoke and the smell of gasoline mixed with oil swirled around her as she cut through several more limbs.

She didn't mind chopping up the tree. It put her in charge of this place. In charge of its destiny. And that felt right.

She and Zoe and Bree had been slowly rebuilding their relationship. Maybe when the house was repaired, their family would be, too.

Charlie, who'd been stacking the wood she cut at the curb, trudged up the driveway, mud streaking his hands and clothes and sweat running down his face. Bits of sawdust clung to his skin and dusted his hair. "Hey, you slacker!" he said. "I've caught up with you."

Fiona set the saw down, opened a cooler

and tossed him a bottle of water, then gave one to Zoe. "We're going to have to hose you off when we're done. You're a mess."

Charlie hooted. "You should talk, dude. You look like a snowman."

She could just imagine. It felt as if every inch of her body was covered with sawdust. "I think it makes a nice statement." She opened a bottle of water and gulped it down. It figured that the weather had become tropical just when there was so much work to be done.

"What kind of statement would that be?"

Jackson. He was walking up the driveway, and her stomach swooped to her toes. Charlie turned to see the twins behind him. After tossing his water bottle into the recycling bin, he ambled over to them.

Fiona tossed her own bottle toward the bin but missed badly. She bent to pick it up and said, "Hey, Jackson." The scene in her basement two nights ago burned in her memory.

"You're quite the sight, Fee."

She ran her hand self-consciously through her hair and sawdust fell like snow. "Don't remind me."

"Hey, it's a good look for you. A chain saw, tank top and shorts." He touched her arm. "How am I supposed to get that picture out of my head?"

"You like dirt and sweat? No wonder you were so comfortable in that basement."

"I wasn't comfortable down there." He gazed down at her, and his eyes gleamed. "Were you?"

"Zoe," she said, irritated that her voice cracked, "you know Jackson, don't you?"

Jackson spun around to where her sister was watching them from the porch. "Hey, Zoe. How're you doing?"

"I'm fine." She stood and walked over. "Looks like you're doing pretty well, too." She glanced from Jackson to Fiona. "Something you wanted to tell me, Fee?"

Fiona turned off the saw. "I told you, Jackson and I are old friends."

"They're the best kind, aren't they?" Zoe said. "You want me to leave you two alone?"

"Bite me, Zo," Fiona said. She used her forearm to wipe the sweat and sawdust off her face. "What's up, Jackson?"

"I need a favor," he said, his expression once again cool and cautious. "I just got an emergency call from the clinic, and I was hoping you could keep an eye on Lindy and Logan for me. They've been fighting so much I don't want to leave them alone at the house, but I don't want them distracting me at the clinic."

"Sure, they can stay here. I'll make them haul branches with Charlie. Hard work should cool their jets."

"Thanks, Fee." He shoved his hands into his pockets. "Is Charlie going to that birthday party later this afternoon? Shannon's party?"

"Is it still on? I forgot all about it."

"Yeah, their house wasn't damaged."

"Then I guess he's going."

"So are the twins. I'll pick all three of them up and take them, since you don't have a car." He glanced at the flattened silver sedan beneath the tree.

"Thanks, Jackson."

He stared at her. "Why are you chopping up the tree? Won't your father's insurance pay to have someone take care of this?"

"If I want to wait a week. But we have to get the house covered up." She gestured to the hole in the wall.

"I'll come back and give you a hand if the emergency turns out to be a quickie." His eyes darkened. "There's something about you and a chain saw I can't resist."

Her hand trembled as she picked up the saw. "Goodbye, Jackson."

"I'll see you later, Fee."

She fired up the saw again. Out of the corner of her eye, she saw her sister's knowing grin. "Don't even start."

"Start what?" But Zoe's obvious excitement ruined her innocent act. "Hey, I'm thrilled. I saw how you looked at him. I'm ecstatic you're staying in Spruce Lake."

"I'm not staying here."

"Are you sure, Fee?"

"Of course I'm sure. I have a show coming up in less than a month. A show I've waited my whole career for." She set the saw down. "Things have changed in Spruce Lake, Zo. I've changed." She smiled. "I like being around my sisters now. But my home is New York."

"What about Jackson?"

"What about him? There's nothing going on between us."

"That's not what it looked like from the cheap seats," Zoe said.

"Later," she said as she spotted Logan and Lindy with Charlie. "Hey, guys," Fiona called. "Thanks for helping."

"Like we had a choice," Lindy said under her breath. Zoe's eyes widened, but Fiona pretended not to hear her.

"You look disgusting," Lindy said.

"Hey," Zoe reprimanded her. "That's pretty rude, Lindy."

"I can't even see her pink hair anymore," Lindy said quickly, looking down.

"It's still there." Fiona brushed her hands through her sawdust-covered hair and the fine particles tickled her nose. "See?"

"Why do you have pink hair, anyway?" Lindy asked. "Are you trying to look like that singer Chantal?"

"Chantal is so fifteen minutes ago. And besides, she stole her look from me," Fiona said, touching the tips of her hair.

"Like you know her," Lindy scoffed.

"As a matter of fact, I do. I designed some jewelry for her."

"So is pink hair supposed to be cool or something?"

"I was making a statement about my art and my disdain for bourgeois values."

"You're weird," Lindy said as she picked up a branch and hauled it toward the curb.

"Lindy!" Zoe was clearly shocked by the child's rudeness.

Fiona just laughed as she watched the three kids argue about where to stack the branches.

If weird was the best Lindy could do, things were looking up.

She was going to miss this. She would miss Charlie and Logan's antics. She'd even miss Lindy and her snarky comments. She glanced at Zoe, who was making her way back to the porch with her phone to her ear. From the way she was smiling and rubbing her stomach, she was talking to Gideon.

She'd miss her sisters, too. And her unborn nieces and/or nephews.

She'd begun to feel like part of a family again. Part of a community. And she'd feel that way even when she was back home in New York.

"MY DAD SHOULD HAVE called by now." Lindy stared out the kitchen window at Parker's house. "Emergencies don't take this long."

"It's only been a couple of hours. Maybe he had to perform surgery," Fiona said. They'd finished chopping up the tree, hosed everyone off except Lindy, who refused to get wet, then walked back to Parker's house, letting their clothes dry in the sun.

"Maybe." Lindy scowled. "It's boring

watching you draw. I'm going to the clinic to check on him."

"Whatever he's doing must be serious, or it wouldn't take so long. You don't want to distract him, do you?"

Lindy shrugged a shoulder as she watched Logan and Charlie run around the yard. Fiona wondered why the girl wasn't out with them.

"You don't have to be polite and stay in here with me," she said, fighting a grin when Lindy rolled her eyes. "Go on outside."

"Boys are stupid," Lindy said. "Logan is a tool, and Charlie is mean."

"Charlie? Mean?" She dropped the pencil she'd been using to sketch with. "What's he done?"

"He and Logan keep saying girls can't play basketball. That our...our chests get in the way." She flopped back in her chair, and Fiona suddenly got it. No wonder Lindy hadn't wanted to get wet. A soggy T-shirt would have made her developing breasts obvious.

And her brother and Charlie had been teasing her about the changes.

"That *is* mean. I'm going to have to kick Charlie's butt."

Lindy started to smile, then she scowled. "Maybe they're right. How would I know?"

Poor Lindy. It had to be tough being the only girl in the house. "Trust me, breasts have nothing to do with basketball." She hesitated. "I know you and your dad have a good relationship, but it's tough to talk to a guy about girl stuff." Fiona kept her gaze fixed on the boys. "I was about your age when my mom died. But I had my sisters, and we all traded information we got from our friends. Do you have an aunt or a cousin you could talk to?"

"My aunts live in St. Louis," she said. "I don't know them very well."

Great. *Okay, McInnes, suck it up. You know what you have to do.* "Well, if you have any questions you don't want to ask your dad, you can ask me while I'm still here."

She expected Lindy to give her a rude answer, but the girl didn't say anything. When Fiona stole a glance at her, she shrugged. "Maybe."

Lindy must really be desperate. "Anytime," Fiona said lightly. "Right now, we're going to show those two jerks how girls play basketball. You ready to kick their butts?"

"Right now?"

"Can you think of a better time?" Fiona's muscles ached from the chain saw, but she was determined to cheer Lindy up. "Come on. Let's take them to school."

They strolled out of the house. "Hey, you two," Fiona called. "I understand you don't think girls can play basketball?"

Charlie turned red. "We were just joking, Aunt Fee."

"We'll see who's joking when we're done with you. Lindy, you take your brother. Charlie is all mine."

Logan tried to dribble around Lindy, giving her a hard hip check, but Lindy stayed on her feet and knocked the ball away from him. When she started to dribble, Logan barreled into her, but she got off a pass to Fiona.

Fiona kept the ball away from Charlie while Lindy positioned herself beneath the basket. Fiona passed her the ball, and Lindy laid it in.

"Sweet," Fiona called, jogging over to fist-bump with Lindy.

They played for twenty minutes, beating the boys by ten points. Fiona was panting and her legs were shaking when they finished, but Lindy's grin as she and Fiona high-fived made up for the aches.

"Our work here is done," Fiona said. "Come on, Lindy. We'll let these dogs lick their wounds in private."

"You look real hot, Aunt Fee," Charlie called as they headed for the house. "You need to cool down."

A blast of cold water hit her back, and Fiona squealed in surprise. When she spun around, Charlie was laughing so hard the hose waved in the air. It soaked Lindy, then splattered the garage door with a hollow sound.

Logan grabbed it away from him and aimed it at his sister, but Lindy charged. Charlie, Logan and Lindy rolled on the ground struggling for the hose, laughing as they got completely soaked and muddy.

Fiona dived in, wrestling Logan for control of the hose. Water blasted up her nose and down her back as she shrieked with laughter. She had just managed to grab it when she heard a car door slam in the driveway.

"It's my dad!" Logan yelled.

They scrambled to their feet, water dripping from their clothes and their hair, as Jackson appeared. Fiona ran to turn off the hose.

"So," Jackson said. "I'm slaving away and what are you guys doing? Having fun. Without me."

A devil she hadn't known she possessed made Fiona turn the faucet back on and aim the hose at Jackson. "There," she said, grinning, as he stared at the wet spot in the middle of his chest. "Now you're having fun, too."

Lindy laughed and gave her a high five, and Logan and Charlie tried to take the hose away from her. "Stop," she told the boys. "I'm not sure how much fun he can take."

"I'm wet," Jackson said.

"Deal with it," she answered as she leaned against the garage.

His eyes darkened as he watched her, and she realized her clothes were plastered to her body. Her light yellow T-shirt probably wasn't hiding much. "I can't believe you did that," he said.

"You looked hot," she said, and all three kids giggled.

He cleared his throat as he looked at Logan and Lindy. "I've been trying to call. I have to do surgery on Mrs. Norden's cat. I'll be a couple more hours, but I should be finished in time to take you guys to the party."

"Okay," they said, and grabbed for the hose.

"That's enough," Fiona called. "Time to clean up. Lindy, you take the first shower. I'll find you some clothes now, and your dad can stop at home before he takes you to the party. Charlie and Logan, roll up the hose, please."

As Fiona headed for the house, Jackson

fell into step beside her. "You are in so much trouble, Fee."

Her breasts tightened. Because of the cold water. "I'm shaking in my shoes."

"You should be. My revenge will be swift and merciless. And you won't see it coming." He skimmed one finger down her arm and stared at her with eyes hot with desire. "It'll come when you least expect it."

"Promises, promises," she said in a low voice. That, she suddenly realized, had been a mistake. You don't poke a sleeping tiger.

AN HOUR LATER, she heard the boys rummaging in the refrigerator as she and Lindy worked in the makeshift basement studio at Parker's.

Fiona looked up from the piece of wax she was carving. She was going to make Lindy a simple, small pendant that would complement the earrings Jackson had bought her. She'd given Lindy a lump of wax to work with and showed her how to carve it in the shape of the design she wanted, but it didn't look as if the girl was really interested.

"Are they coming down here?" Lindy asked.

"I doubt it. They don't care about jewelry." A few moments later she heard the video game come on. "See?"

"Boys suck."

"Yeah, sometimes boys your age do. You'll probably feel a little different when you're older."

Lindy sliced random curls of wax off the cube as she glanced at Fiona. She'd complained that Fiona's T-shirts were too small and retreated to the basement as soon as she showered. Clearly, she was working her way up to saying something. From their conversation in the kitchen earlier and the way Lindy hunched her shoulders in her "too small" T-shirt, Fiona had a pretty good idea what it was.

She continued to work and waited for Lindy to make the first move.

CHAPTER SIXTEEN

LINDY STABBED the dental pick into the wax and dug out a chunk of it. "The thing is, I need a bra," she said, the words coming out in a rush and running together. "The other girls all have them."

Without looking at her, Fiona said, "Yeah? Have you asked your dad to take you shopping for one?" Fiona rounded the inside of the wax mold with a scalpel, then kept carving. Acting as if she had conversations every day about bras with twelve-year-old girls.

"Gross! I can't tell my dad that I need a bra." Lindy was going for scorn and ridicule. But she really sounded sad and alone.

Fiona set the scalpel down. "Yeah, that was a stupid thing to say. I was twelve when my mom died, and I sure wouldn't have asked my dad. What about your mom? Can't she take you?"

"My mom's in England. She's not coming home anytime soon."

"Oh." Poor Lindy. "Um, would you like me to go with you? To help you pick one out?"

"I can go by myself. I know what to buy. I've been reading stuff online." Lindy stabbed at the wax and a chunk went flying. "But I guess you could come if you want."

Reading about buying a bra online? Poor Lindy. "Would you mind?" she asked. "I think it would be fun."

Lindy glanced at Fiona's chest. Her braless chest beneath her work overalls. "You don't even wear bras. How would you know what to get?"

"I wear bras most of the time."

The girl hunched her shoulders. "I don't want you to see me. You know. Without my shirt."

"I wouldn't have to," Fiona said gently. She remembered too well the painful self-consciousness of puberty. "There's a dressing room, just like when you buy other kinds of clothes. You'd go in it by yourself, and I'd hand you the bras. In case you got the wrong size, or something."

Lindy glanced down at her own chest. "Maybe. I guess that would be okay."

"We'll have to make sure it's all right with your dad."

"He'll say yes if *you* ask him."

It sounded like the familiar, surly Lindy, but Fiona saw through the tough act. Lindy would be mortified to ask her father. "Okay, then I'll ask him. Maybe we could go tomorrow."

"A lot of my friends go to Victoria's Secret."

Twelve-year-olds shop at Victoria's Secret? "We can take a look there. But we'll try a couple of different places. We have to find a bra that's comfortable."

"Okay." Lindy looked at the piece of wax she'd been carving. It was a misshapen blob. "This doesn't look like jewelry. This looks stupid."

Fiona took the cube and tossed it into the scrap box. "That's the boring part of making jewelry. Let's use the mold I carved and you can choose a stone to go in it."

TWENTY MINUTES AFTER he'd picked up the kids to take them to the birthday party, Jackson knocked on her door. "Hey, Jackson. What are you doing here?" She opened the door and he walked inside.

Without saying a word, he backed her

against the wall, cupped her face and poured himself into a kiss.

Her legs weakened, but she tried to push him back. "Stop, Jackson. What are you doing?"

"Kissing you." He trailed his mouth down to her neck. "Then I'm going to take off your clothes and make love to you."

"No, you're not," she said against his mouth as she curled her hands into his shirt. She would push him away in a minute.

"You want to take my clothes off and make love to me instead? I'm good with that."

"This is a really bad idea." She arched into his hand when he put it on her breast.

"Yeah, that's what I thought, too." He moved closer, pinning her against the wall.

"We need to talk about this, Jackson," she said, feeling the control slipping away from her. He knew exactly how to touch her, where to touch her, how to kiss her. He knew her body intimately, even after all these years.

"Talk about what?" He kissed her eyelid. "I have condoms." He nuzzled her neck. "I'll respect you in the morning." He unhooked one strap of her overall and pressed his mouth to her breast. "I'm going to die if we don't make love. Okay? Enough talking?"

She moaned at the heat of his mouth on her

breast, the heat building inside her. She slid her hands beneath his shirt and smoothed her hands over his hard muscles, feeling his soft hair against her fingertips.

"You don't want this," she panted.

"You're right." He unhooked the other strap and let the front of her overalls fall to her waist, then put his hands on her breasts. "That's what I've been telling myself since the day I walked into your father's house looking for my kids and saw you." He kissed her again, and she slid her arms around his neck. "I could barely stop myself the other night in the basement. Then you had to go and have a water fight with the kids. How am I supposed to resist you?"

He kissed her again, his body pressing against her from chest to knees. "I can't think of anything but you during the day. I dream about you at night. I need to get you out of my head, Fee."

She'd never forgotten Jackson—his taste, the way he felt, the way he made her feel. No other man had ever touched her the way he had.

Her breasts were swollen and heavy, and she knew her nipples were plainly visible beneath the lightweight T-shirt. She wanted him. Making love to him once wouldn't change anything.

And maybe if they made love, she could put him out of her head, too. Maybe she could go back to New York without the ghosts following her.

"I always loved it when you wore overalls," he said, his voice deeper than usual. "They made me crazy."

"I know." She nipped his neck. "Why do you think I wore them so often?"

"You were a devil, Fee." He touched her collarbone, tracing the graceful swoop across her chest, then his hand drifted down.

He must have felt her surrender, because he kissed her again, deeply, and moved closer. He shaped her breasts, cupping them in his hands. "I want to look at you," he whispered as he drew her shirt over her head and tossed it to the floor. His eyes darkened as he stroked his fingers over her curves as if relearning her. He touched one nipple, caressing it to a tight bud. Then he touched the other one.

She struggled to keep from throwing herself at him. She throbbed in time with his caresses, but he was in no hurry. He moved as if he couldn't get enough of her, as if he was trying to make up for all their lost years.

"My turn," she managed to say. She pulled his shirt off and dropped it. His chest was broader than she remembered and more muscled. Dark blond hair curled over his pecs and arrowed down to disappear into his waistband. When she leaned forward and pressed a kiss to his hot skin, he shuddered.

"Stop, Fee." He set her gently away from him. "I don't have a lot of control right now."

"You say that as if it's a bad thing." She fumbled with the waistband of his jeans trying to undo them.

He caught both of her hands in one of his. "You first. Please." He tugged the overalls lower on her hips.

He peeled the shorts down her legs, kissing as he went. "A thong, Fee? No bra and a thong?" He slid his hands to her hips, knelt down and pressed his mouth between her legs. "What am I going to do with you?"

His voice vibrated against her, and she trembled. "Make love with me, Jackson. Please." She tried to pull him up to her for a kiss. "Now."

He tugged the scrap of silk to one side. "So demanding. Did I tell you I like your bossy side?" He laid her on the couch and kissed her again, and her hips lifted.

Three more strokes of his tongue and she came apart, crying his name. He held her as she shuddered, then lifted her and carried her into the bedroom.

When he set her gently on the bed, she reached for his jeans again. Her hands shook as she unbuttoned him. About to ease the pants down his hips, she stopped in surprise.

"Commando, Jackson?"

"Didn't have time to do the laundry," he said. "God bless emergencies at the clinic."

Smiling, she took him in her hand, loving the heat and hardness of him. She'd missed the fun, the playfulness, the way they'd enjoyed each other's bodies.

"I missed you," she whispered.

He dropped onto the bed next to her. "Goes double for me." He kicked his jeans the rest of the way off, and framed her face with his hands. "I never stopped wanting you, Fee. Never."

Then he was inside her and they were moving together as if they'd never been apart. He murmured her name and she kissed him as if she'd die if she didn't taste him. And when they reached the crest together, she held him tightly as they tumbled over. She couldn't bear to let him go.

They clung together as their breathing

slowed. Twining her legs with his, she nuzzled her face into his neck. "Jackson," she said. "I'm…"

He trailed his fingers over her cheek. "What?"

She didn't have to say it. They both knew this wasn't forever. They both knew she was going back to New York. So she bit his shoulder. "I have another idea. Want to talk about it?"

"I'm about talked out right now. Give me a few minutes."

She grinned into his shoulder. "Okay, smart-ass. But it's about Lindy."

He shifted to look at her. "What about Lindy?"

"She needs a bra."

He stared at her for a moment, then shook his head. "I know we used to talk about anything and everything after we made love, but this is weird, even for us. And how can Lindy need a bra, anyway? She's just a little girl. She doesn't need a bra."

"Technically, no, she doesn't." She wove her fingers through the soft hair on his chest. "But she needs a training bra."

"What the hell is a training bra? She's supposed to train her nonexistent breasts? Train them to do what?"

Tugging at his chest hair, she said, "If you stop being a jerk, I'll tell you."

Jackson shifted so he was sitting against the headboard and sighed. "Lindy's my baby. I don't want her to grow up too early and wear bras."

Fiona wrapped the sheet around herself and sat up. "Yeah, I get that. But she's starting to develop, and she's really self-conscious. And on top of that, Logan and Charlie are teasing her about it."

"What?" His face darkened. "I'll straighten those two out."

"I'll talk to Charlie, but it would help if you did, too. Reinforce the message."

"You got it." He took her hand and played with her fingers. "How do you know all this?"

"Lindy told me."

"What? Lindy confided in you about something so personal?"

"She didn't have anyone else to talk to. Girls are hideously self-conscious when their bodies start to change." She put her hand over his mouth. His lips were firm and warm beneath her fingers. "And before you get all pissy about why she didn't come to you, tell me this. Would you have felt comfortable having that conversation with her?"

"Of course not. But I would have. Better than her going to a stranger."

The barb hit square in the center of her chest. "I'm hardly a stranger."

"You know what I mean," he said impatiently. "She acts as if she hates you."

"She doesn't hate me. She thinks I'm a threat, which is different. But she was feeling raw because of the teasing and I was the only woman around."

"You don't have to take her shopping. You have too much to do with your father's house and getting ready for New York."

But she'd made a promise to Lindy. "I can put aside an afternoon to take her shopping."

"I'll go with her to the store."

"She doesn't want to bra shop with her father." She eased away. "You don't want me to take her, do you?"

"Do you want to?"

"Yes," she said, surprising herself. "I'd like to. But you'd rather I didn't."

"Can you blame me, Fee? You broke my heart. I don't want you breaking my kid's heart."

She'd broken her own heart, as well, but this wasn't the time to get into it. "How am I going to do that by taking her shopping?"

"She'll get attached to you, and then you'll be gone."

"We're talking about a shopping trip, Jackson. A few hours. That's all."

Jackson threw a pillow across the room. "Damn Mallory to hell and back. She should be the one helping Lindy with this stuff."

Okay, this wasn't about her. It was about Lindy's mother. Her shoulders relaxed. "I thought it was odd that Lindy didn't even mention her mom until I asked if Mallory could take her shopping."

"That's because the kids have barely heard from her since she took off. She's only called twice and sent a few e-mails."

"That must be so hard for them. Lindy said she's in England."

"The company she worked for had an opening in their London office. She called me up, told me to take the kids, and left." He sighed. "We never should have gotten married."

"Then why did you?"

"Two reasons. Logan and Lindy. She was pregnant. She told me she was on birth control, but I've often wondered if she lied. Her roommates at the dorm told me Mallory had had a crush on me for a long time. When she turned up pregnant, of course we had to get married."

Coming from a family that defined dysfunctional almost as much as her family did, he would want his kids raised in a stable environment.

He kissed her hand. "Stupid ass thing to do."

"She was pregnant with your children," Fiona said.

He held her hand against his mouth for a moment, then let it go. "I was in love with you. A marriage can't work when the husband is obsessed with another woman. And Mallory never let me forget that. God, she hated you."

Her heart banged against her chest so hard it hurt. "I'm sorry, Jackson."

"It wasn't your fault I slept with Mallory. That's on me. Second biggest mistake I ever made."

She wanted to ask him what the biggest mistake was, but he kept talking.

"Mallory always wanted what she couldn't have. Then when she got it, she was bored. She'd made passes at me when I ran into her on campus, but I told her I was with you. Then you left town and I…I didn't handle it well. She found me one night at the Lake House, drowning my sorrows, and I woke up in her bed the next morning." He pulled the sheet up around her.

"When the twins were born, we were both overwhelmed. I was in vet school by then, and she was working. Logan was colicky. It was a nightmare."

He gave her a sidelong glance. "She got tired of being a mother. That's the only way I can explain it. She got bored with the minutiae of kids, the hard work, the attention they needed. She was always about Mallory first." He scowled. "If she knew you were back in Spruce Lake, she'd probably come back to snatch the kids away from your bad influence."

"I'm sorry," she said softly. Sorry for Jackson, sorry for Logan and Lindy. She wrapped her arms around him and held him tight. "Thank you for telling me. I'm not going to hurt Lindy that way. She's not even sure she likes me. But I can take her shopping for bras. Maybe we'll get manicures and pedicures, too. We'll have a girl's day out. She needs an antidote to all the testosterone she lives with."

"Hey, nothing wrong with testosterone," he said. His fingers drifted down her back, pausing at every bump of her spine.

She shivered. "Absolutely not. It's one of my favorite things."

"Is that a fact?"

"Mmm, hmm." She kissed his ear, smiling when he shuddered. "Whenever you walk into a room, my hormones go on red alert." They always had. Probably always would.

"That's not the only thing that goes on red alert," he said.

"Really." She drew her hand slowly down his chest. "Now that's something I'd like to talk about."

HE WAS IN so much trouble.

He'd thought making love with Fiona would get her out of his system. Let him forget about her and move on.

Instead, he'd fallen for her all over again. How was he going to get over her when she left?

He wasn't going to think about Fiona leaving. Right now, all he wanted to think about was lying next to her, smelling her citrus scent, feeling her smooth skin, relishing the way she wrapped herself around him and held on tightly. Loving the way her hand moved lazily through his chest hair and over his belly.

Then lower.

"I can't believe I'm saying this, but we have to stop," he said as he grabbed her hand

and pressed a kiss to her palm. "Can you hold that thought? We have to get the kids from that party."

"Oh my God." She shot up, untangling herself from him. "I forgot all about Charlie. And Lindy and Logan."

For a little while, he had, too. Nothing and no one had existed besides Fiona. And that was scary. She wasn't supposed to have that much power over him.

She wasn't supposed to get close to his kids. But she was taking Lindy shopping for bras.

What were they going to do when she left in two weeks?

His kids wouldn't have to do a thing, because they'd never know that Fiona was anything more to him than their friend's aunt.

He'd worry about himself later. "I'll get them and pick up pizza," he said. "What do you like?"

She paused while pulling her clothes on. "Is that a good idea? I don't want to upset Lindy right before our girl's day out."

He leaned over and kissed her. "Afraid you won't be able to keep your hands off me?"

Yes. "Just trying to avoid problems."

"It'll be fine." He shrugged into his shorts. Fiona watched him, and his heart ached with longing for her. To hide his reaction, he said, "I didn't know you were such a fan of commando. I'll make a note of it."

"I like a man who can take a hint," she said, equally lightly.

CHAPTER SEVENTEEN

How LONG DID IT TAKE to pick out a bra?

Jackson tossed aside the veterinary journal he was trying to read and paced his living room. What were Fiona and Lindy doing? They'd been gone for almost three hours. The boys were on the driveway shooting baskets, so he had nothing to do but think about Lindy and Fiona.

Mostly Fiona, and the way she'd felt and tasted yesterday.

The dogs scrambled to their feet and began barking, and he heard a car door slam in the driveway. Lindy came bounding up the steps, with two shopping bags.

"Look, Daddy," she said, holding out her hands. Her bright pink fingernails matched the color of one of the bags. "We got manicures. And pedicures." She held up one foot in a flip-flop, and her toenails were the same Pepto-Bismol pink.

"Looks nice, honey," he said. "They're very pink."

"I chose the color myself," she said happily.

He nodded at the bags. "Find what you need?"

She tugged at the blue earring in her ear— her FeeMac earring—and her cheeks turned pink. "Yes."

"Great." He gave her a hug, then watched as she disappeared upstairs. She seemed pretty happy about the afternoon she'd spent with Fiona, he thought uneasily. When he turned, Fiona stood at the door. "Come on in."

She stepped inside and patted Maxine and Kinky, who rushed to greet her. "Mission accomplished."

He led her into the kitchen. "How did it go?"

"It was fun. I had a good time." She grinned. "We bonded over Victoria's Secret lingerie."

"You took my kid to Vic…?"

"Shh. She doesn't want Logan to know. It's okay—they have a section for teens." She wriggled her eyebrows. "And I got a special treat for you."

"Oh, yeah? Are you wearing it?" He wanted to burrow beneath her clothes and find out for himself, but he left his hands on her waist.

"I'm saving it for a special occasion." She

kissed him lightly and stepped away. "The next time we *talk*."

So there would be another time. They hadn't had a chance to discuss what had happened, and he wasn't sure if she thought their lovemaking was a one-time-only deal.

He'd have to figure out a way to get her alone again. Soon. He opened the refrigerator. "You want something to drink? We have lemonade or iced tea."

"Iced tea would be great."

He poured them both a glass, then pushed aside the morning paper and sat at the table. He glanced around the yellow kitchen's cluttered countertops. "Sorry the place is a mess. The kids were supposed to clean it up, but…" He shrugged. He glanced outside to make sure Logan and Charlie were still playing basketball.

"Don't worry about it." She took a sip of the tea and relaxed into the chair. "I need to get to work, but do you want to order some Chinese food first? We can all have dinner together." She smiled. "Lindy has just about decided I don't have horns. I'd like to build on that."

"I'm not sure that's a good idea, Fee."

Her smile faded. "Why not?"

He straightened the newspapers so he didn't have to meet her gaze. "I'd prefer they don't know about us."

"Know what about us, Jackson?"

Damn it. "That we're…together. Dating—no, *not* dating…. Whatever you want to call it."

"Screwing each other? Is that the phrase you're searching for?"

"What do you expect me to say, Fiona? You're only here for a couple more weeks. You want to get all involved with my kids, then break their hearts when you walk away?"

She raised her eyebrows. "Having dinner together would break their hearts?"

No one, not even Mallory, could get him angrier faster than Fiona. "You know damn well what I mean. I'm trying to protect my kids."

"I understand." She stood and slung her purse over her shoulder. "I invited Lindy to help me make a piece for my show. If you don't want her to do that, you can be the one to tell her. I'm not going to be the bad guy."

She walked out of the house, closing the door carefully behind her. *Uh-oh.* He knew Fiona's temper. It would have been better if she'd slammed the door.

He caught up to her as she was getting into the red sedan she'd rented. "Hold on, Fee. Don't walk away angry."

"What? Afraid you're not going to get any more sex?"

"No, damn it." *Yes. But that wasn't the only reason.* "I wasn't trying to hurt you. Maybe I was too blunt. But do you see any reason to tell Logan and Lindy that we're seeing each other?"

"Maybe because we are? And it feels like a lie to be sneaking around, trying to keep it a secret."

"What am I supposed to say? 'Fiona and I are dating for the next few weeks. Then she's leaving again.' How do I explain that?"

"Clearly, you don't." Fiona started the car.

Her phone rang when she was less than a block from Jackson's house. Had he changed his mind? Decided he wanted her to stay for dinner, after all? Heart pounding, she opened her phone.

"Hi, Fiona. It's Helen Cherney."

"Hi, Helen." A wave of disappointment crashed over Fiona as she listened to the attorney. "That's fabulous," she said after a moment.

Helen had called to tell her that Jamie had

some leads on Barb's whereabouts. "Any time frame for when he might know for sure?"

"He's been working double shifts since the tornado, so he hasn't had time to follow up. But I wanted to let you know he hasn't dropped the ball."

"Thanks, Helen. I appreciate the update." Fiona pulled over to the side of the road, her stomach churning. "Let me know if he needs anything from me."

"Will do," Helen said.

Fiona stared at the phone, as if it could give her some answers, then snapped it shut. Okay, it was unlikely she'd find Barb before her show. So she needed to get money from somewhere else. She was almost out of silver, she needed gold and her credit card was maxed out.

The bad news about her finances should have made her fight with Jackson insignificant. Unimportant. But it still mattered.

That wasn't a good sign.

WHEN SHE PULLED into the driveway of Parker's house, the front door was open. Had Bree given Zoe a key?

"Zo?" she called as she walked into the house. "You here?"

"Surprise!" Bree hurried out of the kitchen,

followed by Zoe, and enfolded Fiona in a hug. "We're home."

Fiona hugged her sister tightly. "What are you doing here? You're supposed to be gone for another week."

"Zoe called and told us what happened, so we cut the honeymoon short." She draped one arm over Zoe's shoulder. "We wouldn't make you deal with Dad's house on your own, especially after hearing Zoe's news."

"I'm sorry about your car—"

"Don't be nuts. It wasn't your fault."

She looked behind Fiona. "Is Charlie with you?"

"He's having dinner at the Grants'. He'll be so happy to see you."

"You'll probably be happy to give him back," Bree said.

No, she wouldn't. She'd loved her time with her nephew. "Charlie and I are cool. We've had fun together. But I know he missed you." She hesitated. "So did I."

"I missed you guys, too," Bree said. She hugged Fiona again. "More than I thought I would."

"But you had a great trip, didn't you?"

Her sister's eyes glowed and she gave Fiona a loopy smile. "Beyond wonderful," she said. She turned when Parker came out of the bedroom with two suitcases.

"I'm so sorry you cut it short," Fiona said.

Parker slid his arm around Bree's waist. "We don't have to be in Hawaii to enjoy ourselves."

Yeah, but it wasn't the same with a twelve-year-old boy around. And another adult. "Let me get my stuff out of your room."

"There's no hurry," Bree said, leaning against her husband. "And you don't have to rush back to New York, either. Stay as long as you want."

"And won't that be cozy—you newly-weds, me and Charlie in this tiny house," she said lightly. "I have to get back to New York, anyway. I'll be out of here in a few days."

"We have an extra bedroom," Zoe offered.

"No, Zo, I can't." Her sisters looked so desolate that Fiona hugged them tightly. "It's nothing to do with you guys or Spruce Lake. I have a show coming up and a crisis in my career. I have to get back to take care of it."

"What kind of crisis?" Bree asked. "You have to decide between being on Leno or Letterman?"

That surprised a laugh out of Fiona. "If only. It's not a good crisis. It's a bad one." She explained about Barb and the missing money, about her agent, about the now-critical show. "I have to be in New York with my equipment. I have to be able to talk to the gallery owner, to set up the displays. I have to talk to the bankers who know me and see if I can get a loan."

"A loan?" Zoe frowned. "Why didn't you tell me you needed money?"

"You would have just worried," Fiona said. "You don't need to be worrying right now." She touched her sister's stomach.

"How much money did Barb steal, anyway?" Bree asked.

The figure Fiona gave them made them suck in their breaths. "Wow," Zoe said. "That's a lot."

"Yeah. But I can probably get a loan for enough money to buy the material I need for the show. If I don't have to jump through too many hoops."

"Maybe we could sell Dad's house," Bree said quietly.

"You guys are going to live in there," Fiona protested. "You can't sell it."

"You'll pay us back, and then Parker and I can buy another house. A third of that house belongs to you, you know."

"You're not selling the house," Fiona said

firmly. "I'm not that desperate." She was, actually, but she wouldn't take the house away from Bree. "And besides, I've already had a couple of local contractors give me estimates for repairing it."

Bree frowned. "Really? You should have waited and let us hire the contractor."

"I couldn't wait," Fiona said. "There's a hole in the kitchen. The back wall is missing. Do you want every raccoon in Spruce Lake to make himself at home in there?"

"I wanted to pick out the stuff in my new kitchen."

Fiona took a deep breath. This was the point in the discussion where she usually lost her temper and stalked out of the house.

"You can still do that," she said slowly. "We didn't talk about cabinets and counters and all that stuff. I just wanted to get someone started so you wouldn't have to wait as long."

Bree hugged her. "Thanks, Fee. For taking care of it."

"I guess we're making progress," Fiona said. "I'm going to miss you guys. A lot." She'd miss Charlie, too, and Zoe and Gideon's babies.

"We'll miss you, too," Zoe said.

"I want you to stay," Bree said. "Can't you make your jewelry in Spruce Lake?"

"It's not as simple as just making jewelry. I have a company to run. I can't do that long distance." She'd already damaged it by staying here for so long.

"And you want to go back, don't you?" Zoe asked. "That's where you belong."

"Yeah, it's where I belong. Every part of my life is in New York." Jackson's face flashed into Fiona's mind. "But I'll be back to visit. Frequently. And you can come to New York. You'll come for my show, won't you? Please?"

"We wouldn't miss it," Bree assured her.

"Of course we wouldn't." Zoe hesitated. "But what about Jackson?"

"I'll invite him, too," Fiona said. But her chest tightened.

"That's not what I meant. I thought you two had something going on."

"Jackson Grant?" Bree asked. "And Fee?"

Zoe nodded. "Big-time."

"It's nothing," Fiona said, but her heart called her a liar.

"Didn't look like 'nothing' to me," Zoe said.

"Trust me, it is. He doesn't even want to tell his kids we're going out."

Neither of her sisters looked convinced. Fiona sighed. "Long-distance relationships never work."

Zoe and Bree stared at her for a long moment, then glanced at each other. Then they both looked back at her. "You're in love with Jackson, aren't you?" Bree said.

Was she that transparent? Or was it the triplet ESP again? "I don't think I ever fell out of love with him," Fiona said quietly. "But it doesn't matter. I chose a different path almost thirteen years ago, and I don't know how to get us on the same one now."

"You'll figure something out." Zoe sounded confident.

Fiona wasn't so sure.

"HEY, GIRLS, I have something to tell you," Fiona said after basketball practice on Tuesday. She'd been coaching the girls since Jackson's assistant for Lindy's team had broken his ankle. She hadn't wanted to do it, but Jackson had been desperate.

"I have to leave," she told them. "I have to go back to New York." The chorus of "No's" and "You can'ts" didn't make her feel any better. She hadn't expected it to be so hard to tell them she was leaving. She hadn't expected that she'd miss them after she'd gone.

But she would.

"Dr. Grant is a great coach," she said.

"You guys are going to kick some butt during the season."

"But we want you to be our coach," Rachel said.

"Sorry, Rach. I can't stay. How about if I make you some team jewelry? A team pendant to match your jerseys. When you find out what color they are, let me know."

She watched the girls straggle out of the gym, followed by the boys. Lindy stared at her, then turned and heaved the ball toward the hoop. "Are you still coming over tonight to help me with that piece for the show?" Fiona asked her.

"Yeah," she said without looking. "They all want you to stay."

Fiona wanted to ask if Lindy did, too, but decided not to push it. "I wish I could."

She felt Jackson come up behind her and put his hands on her shoulders. "Get your stuff together, guys. I need to talk to Fiona."

JACKSON WATCHED Logan and Lindy, who were now playing Horse with Charlie, and drew Fiona to one side. She wore tight black shorts that hugged her legs, emphasizing every curve. Her tank top was snug, too, and when she lifted the hem to wipe the sweat off her face, he caught a glimpse of smooth white skin.

Hell. He hadn't been able to keep his eyes off her during practice. They hadn't had any time together since Sunday. It was only Tuesday, and he was already going nuts.

He needed to see her again. And not just because he wanted to make love with her. He wanted to spend time with her. Talk to her.

He wanted to be with her.

That made him a real idiot. She was going back to New York, and that was good. He wasn't ready for a relationship. He wasn't ready to put his kids through that particular wringer.

"When are you leaving?" he asked.

"In a few days. It would have cost too much money to fly back immediately."

"Can we get together before you go?" He couldn't bear the thought of not being able to hold her one more time.

"Yes," she whispered. "Bree and Parker already said they'd watch the kids."

"I'll call you tonight and we'll figure out a plan." After the kids were in bed.

"Lindy wanted to work on that piece I'm making for the show tonight. Is that okay?"

"Sure. In fact, why don't you take her with

you now, and I'll bring dinner over later." He ached to touch her, but he kept his hands at his sides. "You two will need to keep up your strength while you're working."

"We'll see you later."

CHAPTER EIGHTEEN

"FIONA! Someone's at the door." Lindy sounded exasperated as she scooped the barking Annabelle off the floor. "Can't you hear that?"

"Sorry," Fiona said as she dropped the piece of silver. "It's probably your dad. He was going to bring us food." She looked at the piece of jewelry that Lindy had been carefully smoothing with a file. "You're doing a nice job."

"Thanks." Lindy hurried up the basement stairs, followed by Fiona.

"Sorry," Fiona said as she let Jackson and Logan into the house. "I didn't hear the door."

"She doesn't hear a *thing* when she's working." Lindy rolled her eyes.

Jackson set a pizza box on the kitchen table. "The delivery boy is here."

"What are you guys doing down there?" Logan asked, staring into the basement.

"Lindy, you want to show him? Just be careful of the soldering iron. It's still hot."

"Duh. You think I'm three years old?" Lindy put the dog down and clattered down the basement stairs, followed by Annabelle.

"I guess she hasn't become a complete pod person," Fiona said.

"Yeah. I'd be afraid she was sick if she didn't get a zinger in every now and then." Jackson looked around the kitchen. "Where's Bree and Parker and Charlie?"

"They went out to dinner, then they're meeting with the contractor who's going to fix the house." Logan and Lindy's voices drifted up from the basement. "They offered to take your kids out to dinner tomorrow night."

"Is that right?" He took her hand and tugged her closer. "Will they make it a long dinner?"

"They can probably stretch it out a couple of hours." Not long enough to say her goodbyes to Jackson, but it was all she was going to get.

"It's a date."

The words pierced her heart. "I'll mark you down," she said lightly.

"You do that." He tucked his finger into the neck of her T-shirt. "I can't wait until tomorrow," he whispered.

He nipped at her lower lip and smoothed his hands over her hips. When he pulled her against him, she felt the hard ridge of his erection against her abdomen.

She slid her arms around his neck and kissed him, and he kissed her back as if he couldn't get enough of her. As if she was as essential to him as his next breath.

Fiona trembled against him, her legs weak, her heart pounding. Was he going to miss her as much as she was going to miss him?

"Fiona? Where's the small needle-nose—"

Jackson quickly set Fiona away from him.

"Fiona will be right down, Lindy."

Fiona turned to look, but Lindy was already running back down the stairs.

"Damn it." Jackson shoved his hand through his hair. "What the hell was I thinking?"

"Did she see…?"

"Hell, yes, she saw. God." He paced around the kitchen. "What am I going to tell her?"

Fiona wrapped her arms around herself, suddenly cold. "You haven't told them."

"No, I haven't. What's the point? You're leaving."

"What if I wasn't? What would you tell them then?"

He stared at her for a moment, and she

thought she saw fear in his eyes. "That's irrelevant, because you *are* leaving. I have to talk to her."

He ran down the stairs, and Fiona stood in the kitchen, her heart aching, as she listened to the low murmur of their voices. After several minutes, Jackson returned to the kitchen, followed by Logan. Jackson's son gave her a speculative look, but he didn't say anything.

"She says she's fine." Jackson didn't look at her. "She says she knows her mom isn't coming back, so who cares who I kiss. I offered to take her home, but she says she wants to stay and work on the jewelry."

Oh, God. Was she supposed to sit with Lindy and act as if nothing had happened?

"Fine. We'll call you when she's ready to go."

"Fee…"

"I think you should leave now, Jackson." Before he could say anything else.

Before he could hurt her anymore.

When the front door shut behind him, she took a breath and headed downstairs.

Lindy was sitting in the extra chair at the worktable, bent over the piece of silver that would hold a moonstone, her hair hiding her face. She was using a fine file to rasp away the tiny burrs on the bezel. She didn't look up when Fiona sat beside her.

"Do you want to talk about what happened upstairs?"

Lindy shook her head, but the file slipped and left a red mark on her thumb.

She hesitated. "I care about your father. A lot."

Lindy kept working, but her knuckles whitened on the file. After a few moments, Fiona picked up the design sketch she'd been working on, but she could hardly bear to look at it. She'd been thinking about Jackson when she started it, she realized. The sketch almost looked like a sun, with streams of light spilling out of it. Alive. Glowing. How she'd felt until a few minutes ago.

Lindy set the file and bezel down on the workbench. "I need to go to the bathroom."

"Okay."

Lindy scooped up Annabelle and walked up the stairs. Fiona tried to muster some enthusiasm for the design. But all she saw was Jackson's face. His reaction when she'd asked what he'd do if she stayed in Spruce Lake. The fear he'd tried to hide.

Is this what he'd been planning all along? Make her fall in love with him, then dump her the way she'd dumped him?

No. Jackson was the least vindictive person she knew. And he'd only been telling the truth. She wasn't staying in Spruce Lake. She was leaving in less than a week.

But he didn't have to be so happy about it. So relieved.

So scared that she might change her mind.

She reached for the sketchbook. Her source of comfort for so long. She started to draw.

Toenails clicked on the stairs and Annabelle trotted over to her and licked her hand. Fiona tossed the sketch of heavy lines and downward curves onto the table. "Did you abandon Lindy?" she asked the dog. Annabelle wagged her tail and settled in the bed next to Fiona's chair.

Lindy had been in the bathroom for a long time, she realized uneasily.

Shoving away from the table, she ran upstairs, calling, "Lindy? Are you okay?"

There was no answer.

"Lindy?" Fiona hurried to the bathroom. The door was ajar, and Lindy wasn't inside. "Lindy? Where are you?"

Fiona frantically searched the house, but

it didn't take long to confirm what she already knew.

Lindy was gone.

"JACKSON?" Fiona struggled to control her breathing. She'd run through the house again, then searched outside. "Lindy ran away. Is she at home?"

"Ran away?"

So she hadn't gone home. Fiona gripped the phone so hard her fingers ached. "She said she had to go to the bathroom. When I checked on her, she was gone."

"I'll be right there." The line disconnected, and Fiona rushed into the backyard. The sky was darkening, and it wasn't only because it was dusk. Black clouds were gathering in the west. "Lindy?" she called. But only the distant rumble of thunder answered her.

She froze. A storm was coming. She needed to get her pills.

But they'd make her groggy. And she needed to search for Lindy. She ran into the house and shoved the small vial into her pocket.

There was no place for a kid to hide in Parker's sparsely landscaped yard. Her fingers shook as she pressed the keypad on Parker's garage door. "Lindy?"

The garage was empty.

She ran down the sidewalk, calling the girl's name. The wind picked up and leaves rustled on the maple trees that lined the street. The next time thunder rumbled, she wrapped her fingers around the pill bottle. She was a block away from the house. She could do this.

Jackson's truck turned down the street. He screeched to a stop, and he was out and running, leaving the truck door open behind him.

"Are you sure she's not hiding inside?" he called.

Fiona ran to meet him. "I've already searched three times. The garage, too. She's not here."

He hauled her inside. "What the hell did you say to make her run away?"

"I didn't say a thing! I asked her if she wanted to talk about what she'd seen. She didn't answer. Then I told her I cared about you. She didn't say anything to that, either. She said she had to go to the bathroom, and the next thing I knew, she was gone."

He looked behind the chairs and the drapes, as if she had somehow missed Lindy. As if she wasn't really gone, just hiding.

"You didn't hear her walking out of the house? You didn't hear the door close?"

She shook her head, fighting tears. She smoothed the label on the vial with her thumb. It was almost dark. A storm was coming. She had to control the panic.

"How long was it? Between when she went upstairs and you realized she was gone?"

"I'm not s-sure," she said. "Ten minutes? Fifteen?" Maybe more. She'd been so caught up in her pain she hadn't noticed the clock.

"You were working on your jewelry, weren't you?" He slammed his fist into the wall. "You were doing your zombie thing and didn't notice my kid walking out of the house."

"What zombie thing? What are you talking about?"

"The way you get when you're working," he said, his voice rising. "Like you're dead to everything but what's in your head. You don't hear the door, the phone, people walking around. You don't notice a damn thing. Including my daughter. Who you were supposed to be watching."

"We'll find her," Fiona said. She reached for him, but he backed away. She curled her fingers into her palms. "I'll call the girls on the basketball team," she said after a moment. "Maybe she went to a friend's house."

"You call the team." The wind gusted through the open front door. "I'll call her other friends."

It took fifteen minutes. No one had seen Lindy.

"Let's drive around," Fiona said, desperate to be doing something. Desperate to distract herself. Staying in the house while Lindy was missing was agony. "There must be places she likes to go. Where does she hang out?" She grabbed her keys and jiggled them in her hand.

"There's a park where she and Logan used to play basketball. You stay here in case she shows up."

"Why don't you let me drive? That way you can concentrate on looking for her."

"Let you drive? When you're on the edge of a panic attack? Do you think I'm an idiot?"

So he'd noticed. She wiped her hands down the sides of her overalls. "I can't stay here and do nothing. Driving would take my mind off the storm."

"All right," he finally said. "Let's go."

As they drove slowly down the street, Jackson opened the window and called, "Lindy!" He called again and again, but the only sound was the wind. She flinched when a bolt of lightning flashed in the distance. Jackson gripped the armrest and stared into the darkness. But he didn't touch her.

He didn't look at her or say anything, either. He didn't have to. Guilt pressed down on her, heavy and smothering. Her heart pounded and her chest got tight as she drove slowly through the town. Panic from the storm mixed with fear for Lindy until she couldn't breathe.

It was almost completely dark, and shadows blended and shifted. A shrub looked like a girl, crouching near the ground. The corner of a garage might have hidden a child in the darkness. Lindy hadn't been at the basketball park, or any of the others they'd checked.

Jackson's phone rang, and he glanced at the screen. "It's the library." He took the call. "Jackson Grant."

After listening for a moment, his shoulders slumped. "Thank God. You're a lifesaver, Evelyn. Don't let her leave. I'll be right there."

He closed his eyes and shut the phone. "She's at the library. She's been on a computer." He stared out the car window. "I should have thought of the library."

"Why did she go there?" She rolled her shoulders and her tense muscles protested.

"Mallory used to take her to the library. It was their thing. They went once a week, then they'd go get an ice cream cone or a root beer float. Hot chocolate during the winter."

"Poor Lindy."

"She misses her mom," he said.

"And she's afraid of losing her dad, too. That's why she's so upset about you kissing me."

He shrugged one shoulder. "Maybe."

She turned the corner onto Main Street, and he tensed. "Where are you going?"

"The library, of course."

"No. Go back to your place. I'll go alone."

She turned at the next street, swallowing the lump in her throat. "I suppose that's smart."

She had barely stopped the car when he got out. "I'll talk to you later," he said, but he didn't look at her. The first drops of rain fell as she stood in the driveway, watching his taillights get smaller until they disappeared around a corner.

What was there to talk about? She'd lost his child.

CHAPTER NINETEEN

SHE KNOCKED SOFTLY at Jackson's front door, her nerves jittery, her hands shaking. The light from his living room was reflected in the slick of water on the driveway. It had been three hours since he'd dropped her off, but he hadn't called, and she hadn't been able to sleep. She wanted to make sure Lindy was okay.

He opened the door, clearly tired. "Fee. What are you doing here?"

"How's Lindy?"

He hesitated, then stepped aside. "Come on in. She's in bed. Logan is, too."

He ushered her into the kitchen, then pulled the pocket door that separated it from the dining room. "She's okay. She was really quiet and clingy." He rubbed his face. "She said she knew it was wrong to take off, but she wanted to think about her mom. And she didn't want to be around you. She said you were just being nice to her to get to me."

"You told her that wasn't true, didn't you?"

There was a long pause. "I didn't discuss you at all. There was no reason to."

"No reason?" She shoved her hands into her back pockets so he wouldn't see them trembling. "She caught us kissing and you had nothing to say?"

"You're going to be gone in less than a week. Why does it matter?"

"So you let Lindy think I was using her to soften you up." It felt like a slap in the face.

"What difference does it make, Fiona?" he said impatiently.

"You want your children to think I was manipulating them? That I'm cold and uncaring? That I don't care about them?" She took a deep breath.

"Of course not. There's no reason for Logan and Lindy to think of you at all."

"Is that what *you* think of me, Jackson?"

He shrugged. "I think you're part of my past. Someone I cared about a long time ago." He didn't meet her gaze. "Someone who's not part of my life anymore."

"What about 'I can't wait until tomorrow'?"

"That had nothing to do with my kids."

"I don't think it's so easy to separate the two," she said slowly. "If you're lying to your kids about our relationship, what else are you lying about?" She stood and paced the small kitchen. "Is this about revenge? About making me want you again, then saying so long when I leave?"

"You were the one who was clear that you weren't sticking around. You can't have it both ways, Fiona. You're determined to go back to New York, and I'm not going to stop you. That has nothing to do with my kids. Or did you think I was going to beg again? Plead with you to stay? Not going to happen."

"Isn't there some kind of middle ground?" She didn't want to walk away and forget about Jackson. "Some way we can compromise?"

"How would we do that? Are you asking me to give up my veterinary practice and move to New York with you? I can't do that. And I don't hear you offering to make a change. Are you willing to move back to Spruce Lake permanently?"

She dropped her gaze.

"I didn't think so."

"You don't even want to try and work something out. But what happens when you meet someone you want a relationship with? Someone who *will* be around? Logan and

Lindy aren't going to trust any woman in your life."

"My kids don't need to worry that some woman will take their place in my life," he said, crossing his arms.

"Lindy is obviously worried about it. Have you talked to her about the divorce? About her mother being gone?"

"Don't tell me what my daughter thinks. Or how to raise her." He slammed shut a cabinet door that had been left open, and it bounced open again. "You don't know squat about raising kids."

She told herself the anger in his voice wasn't directed at her. There couldn't be anything more frightening for a parent than having their child disappear.

"I know enough to realize you take wonderful care of your kids. But they lost their mother. That's a lot to deal with." The picture of Lindy sitting alone in the library, crying for her mom, broke her heart.

"As bad as Mallory was, she never lost them."

She sucked in a breath. "That's not fair."

"You were watching her. She left the house. You didn't notice she was gone because you

were working. Too absorbed to notice anything else."

"She's twelve years old. She's not a toddler
who has to be watched every minute. She's
old enough to go to the bathroom by herself,
for God's sake."

"You knew she was upset. You should have
been paying attention to her, not your damn
jewelry." He picked up a soda can on the
counter and hurled it across the room at a recycling bin. It missed and rolled across the
floor.

She bit her lip. "I'm not the only one at
fault here, Jackson," she said when she was
sure her voice would be steady. "If you'd told
her we were involved, she wouldn't have been
shocked. Maybe she wouldn't have run away."

His eyes were as flat and cold as the stones
at the bottom of Spruce Lake. "Just like it was
my fault you ran?"

"It all comes back to that, doesn't it? That
I took off all those years ago. That I'm going
to hurt you again."

Damn straight. "I don't give a damn about
myself. I survived you once and I'll survive
you this time, too. But you're not going to
hurt my kids." He nodded at the refrigerator,
at Logan's and Lindy's school pictures.

"You're not going to break their hearts the way you broke mine."

"You let me walk away."

"Is that what it was?" Anger was better, he told himself. Better than the fear. "We were playing a game? See how many hoops you could make me jump through? I begged you to stay, Fiona."

"I left because I had to go. I had to get away from Spruce Lake and my father. I had to go to New York to learn my craft. You never understood that. You never understood how critical that was."

"I understood it was more important than I was." He'd been shattered when she left. And he'd never really recovered.

"I would have regretted it my whole life if I didn't go to New York and follow my dream."

"We had different dreams, Fiona." The pain was still an open wound.

"We're both adults now, Jackson. Can't you see a way to make it work?" She touched his arm. "Do you want me to beg? All right, I'm begging."

He would have given anything to hear those words twelve years ago.

"That's supposing we want to make it work." He walked to the window and stared outside, seeing nothing but darkness. "Do you, Fiona?"

"Yes," she said slowly. "I do. I don't want to walk away from you again."

"So you're staying in Spruce Lake?" His heart began to race.

"I *have* to go back home."

He shrugged. "Don't say I didn't ask."

"What about you, Jackson? Do you want to make this work? Or do you want to feel righteous? Because that's all I'm seeing right now."

"Righteous? No. I'm a guy who learned not to trust you. And I'm a guy who has children to protect now. So unless you can tell me how this is going to work, I'm not buying what you're selling."

"I don't know how it will work. But we could figure it out together."

"No, thanks. You're not jerking me around again."

"You don't trust me to love you enough. That's why it has to be either-or," she said slowly. "You didn't trust me then, either."

"You left me. You proved I was right."

She hesitated. "The other day, you said marrying Mallory was your second biggest mistake. What was the biggest one?"

"I thought it was not running after you.

Not fighting for you. I guess I was smarter than I thought."

She recoiled as if he'd hit her.

Good. He'd intended his words to hurt.

"Nothing's changed, has it?" Her low voice touched a spot inside him he'd sworn she'd never touch again.

He looked away.

She blinked twice, as if trying to hold back tears. "Okay. I get it. Tell Lindy and Logan…" She swallowed hard. "Tell them I'll miss them."

She turned and walked out.

JACKSON RUBBED his chest as he stood at the door and watched Fiona's car drive away. She wanted to make it work. Wanted to be with him.

And he'd told her to get lost.

"Dad?"

Lindy was at the foot of the stairs. Her pajama pants were rumpled and her T-shirt was twisted around her waist. Her hair stood up in clumps. "Hey, sweetheart. What's wrong?"

"I heard you and Fiona."

Damn it. "Sorry we woke you up, punkin. Go on back to bed."

She sat on the lowest step. "What did she

mean about being with you? I thought she lived in New York."

"She does. And she's going back there in a couple of days."

Lindy frowned. "Did she want you to go with her?"

He wasn't about to discuss Fiona with his daughter. "I'm not going anywhere, Lindy. Fiona and I were having an adult conversation. Okay? Now go to bed."

"Do you miss Mom?"

He lowered himself to the stair next to his daughter. "I know you miss her a lot, Lindy. I know that's why you went to the library tonight. Because that's where you went with your mom."

"I wish Mom hadn't left."

"I know." He wrapped his arm around his daughter's shoulder. "She misses you, too."

Lindy rested her chin on her knees. "No, she doesn't. If she did, she'd call us more often."

"She's really busy with her job," Jackson said. *Damn you, Mal.*

Lindy looked at him with eyes far older than her years. "She would call us if she wanted to."

"There's a time difference," he said. "She's six hours ahead of us."

"That's lame." She gave him a scornful look. "*You're* lame."

"That's me," he said. "Cursed with terminal lameness."

She slugged his shoulder. "Don't be a jerk, Dad." She leaned against him. "I e-mailed Mom," she said in a small voice. "I told her you were going out with Fiona."

He groaned inwardly, then wrapped his arm around Lindy and pulled her against his side. If anything would bring Mallory back into her kids' lives, it was the news he'd gotten together with Fiona. "Why did you do that, honey?"

"I wanted to talk to her about it. I wanted to know what she thought." She dug her toe into the carpet. "I guess I wanted her to tell me it was okay, you know?"

Mallory would never do that.

Although it didn't matter now, because Fiona was gone.

"Your mom doesn't need to tell you who to like and who not to like. You can figure that out for yourself."

"It felt bad when I started to like Fiona," Lindy muttered. "I thought it meant I didn't love Mom."

"That's not true. Your mom will always be

your mom. Nothing can change that. You care about them in different ways."

Lindy didn't answer. The clock ticked in the kitchen, marking each second that passed. Outside, headlights sliced through the night as a car drove down the street and past the house.

Finally Lindy asked, "Are you going to marry Fiona?"

"Nobody said anything about getting married." And no one would, now that he'd told her to leave.

"Are you still going out with her?"

"We were never really going out."

Lindy frowned. "You were kissing her."

"I lo…like Fiona. But it's complicated."

Lindy nestled against his chest, her hair tickling his nose. She was cold, so he rubbed her arm. They sat together, neither of them speaking.

Finally she shifted so she was looking at him. "The girls on the team like her. They think she's chilling. And she's an awesome coach."

"I thought you hated her."

Lindy smoothed the leg of her pajamas. "She let me help her make jewelry. That was fun. And she's going to use the pendant I helped her make in her show. She said it would be a big hit."

"Yeah?" Fiona, who was so single-minded about her work, had let a kid work on one of the pieces for her important show? "That's, uh, nice of her."

Lindy shrugged her shoulder again. "So I decided she was okay."

"Then why did you take off on her?"

"I was mad you didn't tell me you guys were going out." She twisted her hair around a finger and looked away. "And I told you already, I was upset because if you were kissing Fiona it meant Mom wasn't coming back."

"Mom was never coming back," he said gently. "Whether I kissed Fiona or not."

"I guess I knew that. But I was still hoping, you know? Until I saw you guys together."

Jackson dropped a kiss on Lindy's head. "I know this is hard for you, baby."

"I'm not a baby, Dad," she said, pushing away from him.

"You'll always be my little girl. Even when you're forty."

"You're such a dork," Lindy said, and he smiled.

They sat on the stairs and he listened to his daughter breathe. She and Logan were miracles. The best part of him. He was only protecting them, he told himself. Only trying to make sure they didn't get hurt.

Liar. He was protecting himself.

Lindy stood up. "Can I go back to Fiona's tomorrow and finish the pendant? I should tell her I'm sorry I took off."

"Fiona's leaving."

"Because you were mean to her."

"Yeah, I was a little mean. But that's not why she's leaving." He'd been more than a little mean. He'd hurt her. Deliberately. "She has to get ready for that show."

"I wanted to help her."

"You can call her tomorrow and wish her good luck."

She nodded. "I'll apologize, too." She trudged up the stairs to her bedroom.

He should have had this conversation with his kids a long time ago, he thought as he listened to his daughter's door close. Fiona had been right about that.

He stared at the phone but didn't pick it up.

FIONA PACKED her clothes methodically, folding each shirt and pair of pants. Her hand lingered over her cutoff overalls. Then, blinking hard, she put them in her suitcase and covered them with a stack of T-shirts.

"Stay a couple more days," Bree said. "Don't leave while you're upset."

"It'll be better when I go home. Better to keep busy."

Bree turned her around and hugged her. "Zo and I will make his life a living hell. We'll make a voodoo doll and stick needles where they'll hurt the most. And if he comes sniffing around, we have knives. I'm sure we can find creative uses for them."

There was a rapping at the front door, and she heard Parker open it. "Come on in, Zoe. I was just heading over to my lab at the college. They're starting to talk about needles and sharp instruments, and I have a weak constitution."

Fiona choked on a laugh as Zoe flopped onto the bed, spilling her carefully folded clothes onto the floor. "What's wrong?" She wore a pair of pajama bottoms and what was clearly one of Gideon's shirts. "What happened?"

"Rat bastard Grant broke her heart," Bree said. "We're making our plans."

Zoe enfolded her in a hug. "Tell me."

A half hour later, a cup of tea in her hands, Fiona sat at Parker's utilitarian kitchen table with her sisters. "I can't believe you guys got up in the middle of the night for me."

"I was supposed to let you cry?" Bree said.

"I don't cry." Her nose was still stuffy and her eyes were swollen.

Jackson was the only one who'd ever been able to make her cry.

Instead of the smart answer she expected, Bree smoothed a tear from her cheek. "You never cried, even when Dad was telling you your jewelry sucked. Zo and I left you alone with Dad, but we're not abandoning you again. We're going to get through this together." She scowled. "And Jackson Grant is a jackass who doesn't deserve you."

Fiona felt her eyes watering again. "Jeez, you two. What am I supposed to say to that?"

"Say you won't go back to New York and forget about us," Zoe said quietly. "Say you'll be part of our lives, and you'll let us be a part of your life. That *here* will be home for you."

"Spruce Lake *is* home. It just took me awhile to realize it. You'll get sick of seeing me, I'll be here so often. And you're still coming to New York for my show, aren't you?"

"We wouldn't miss it," Bree assured her. She looked at Zoe. "We have something we want to say, and I guess this is as good a time as any."

Zoe squeezed her hand. "We have your

money, Fee. What you need to buy the materials for your show."

"What?" Fiona looked at them, confused. "Did Jamie call? Did he find Barb?"

"Nope. It's a loan from us," Bree said. "Until you find Barb."

"You guys don't have that kind of money," Fiona said, shocked. "And even if you did, I couldn't take it."

"I told you that's what she would say," Zoe said to Bree. Then Zoe turned back to Fiona. "It's a loan, Fee. Just like you were going to get from the bank, but without the paperwork and hassle. When you get your money from Barb, you can pay us back."

"Parker gave me some money to start a dance studio," Bree said. "But I won't be ready to open it for a while. I have a lot of work to do first. So the money would be just sitting in the bank. You might as well be using it."

"And I have some savings," Zoe added. "We're not going to let you say no. So be smart and give in gracefully."

"I don't know what to say." She thought she'd cried herself dry, but tears welled in her eyes again.

"Say thank you," Bree said. "Then go kick ass in New York."

CHAPTER TWENTY

FIONA PUT the stamp on the last invitation to her gallery show, then added it to the pile. Then she picked it up again.

Jackson, Logan and Lindy Grant. She stared at the address, wondering if she should send it. Wondering if he would come.

Wondering why she was getting her hopes up. He'd made it clear how he felt. She'd been back in New York for a week and hadn't heard from him.

She hadn't called him, either, she reminded herself.

She shoved the invitation into the middle of the pile to make it harder to chicken out. Then, before she could change her mind, she slipped on her shoes and hurried down the stairs to the mailbox in front of the bakery on the next block.

He wouldn't come. He couldn't leave his

practice. The kids were in school. They had cross-country practice.

There were a lot of reasons he wouldn't show up.

And only one reason he would.

As she hurried back to her studio, she tried to put the invitation out of her mind. It was done, and it couldn't be undone.

He'd either show up, or he wouldn't.

JACKSON DUMPED the mail on the kitchen counter without looking at it. Bills, ads and donation requests. None of them needed his attention right now.

"Hey, guys, time to eat," he called. He opened the box on the kitchen table and stared at the cheese and pepperoni pizza. Fiona's favorite.

He slammed the lid back down on the box. He shouldn't be feeding his kids pizza for dinner. He'd start cooking regularly. In the meantime, he'd make a salad to go with this.

As he was chopping a green pepper, Lindy came in. "Set the table for me, please," he said.

"Okay." She opened the cabinet, then looked at the counter. "What's this?"

"The mail."

"No, I mean this thing." She studied a cream-colored envelope. "It's from New York!"

He gripped the knife more tightly. Then he set it carefully on the counter. "Let me see it."

It had to be from Fiona. He hesitated before he opened it. Did he want to read a letter from her? Did he want to hear how well she was doing in the city? Back where she belonged?

Lindy was watching him expectantly, so he forced himself to open it. A cream-colored card that matched the envelope slid out.

He scanned the card, then closed his fist around it.

"What is it, Dad? Is it from Fiona?"

"It's an invitation. To her show. The gallery probably sent it out."

"Let me see it." Lindy snatched it out of his hand, along with the envelope, and uncrumpled it. "It's addressed to all of us. Can we go, Dad? I want to see her show. I want to see the pendant we made together."

Jackson took the invitation back and tore it into tiny pieces, then dropped them into the wastebasket. "We can't go, honey. You have school that day, and I have to work."

Lindy's face fell. "But she wants us there. She sent us an invitation."

"Whoever owns the gallery sent it out," he

said. "She probably doesn't even know they did."

"She had to give them our address," Lindy argued. "So she must know."

"We can't go, Lindy," he said, his voice rising. "Don't ask again."

The plates clattered as she tossed them on the table. Then she grabbed silverware and practically threw it at the plates. "The table's set," she said as she flounced out.

Dinner was tense and silent. Logan glared at him as he shoveled pizza into his mouth and pushed his salad away. His sister had clearly told him about the invitation.

Lindy only played with her food. She finally stood and stalked away from the table without asking to be excused, daring him to correct her.

"Damn it, Fee," Jackson muttered as he put the dishes in the dishwasher. "How come she's on your side?"

He retreated to his home office to write payroll checks and order drugs and supplies. While he was working, he heard Lindy rummaging in the kitchen. Probably eating the leftover pizza she'd conspicuously ignored at dinner.

When he went in to kiss her good-night

after she was in bed, she pretended to be asleep. He stood next to her bed for a moment, wondering what to say, then he spotted it on her desk.

The invitation from Fiona. Lindy had fished it out of the garbage can and taped it together. The envelope was beneath it.

He traced his finger over the printed *Fiona McInnes requests the honor of your presence,* his finger catching on the edges of the tape. It sounded like a wedding invitation.

Which was just about right, he thought. She was married to her damned career.

She didn't have room in her life for a family.

For him.

But she'd wanted to, that voice reminded him. She'd told him she didn't want to say goodbye.

He picked up the invitation and started to leave the room, but Lindy shot up in bed. "You can't have that. Put it back."

"What are you talking about?" He glanced at her, and her eyes narrowed.

"The invitation. You threw it away, so it's not yours anymore. It's mine now." She crawled to the end of the bed and held out her hand. "Give it to me."

"What do you want this for?" He held it up.

It felt fragile, as if it would fall apart if he wasn't careful.

She snatched it from his hand, then set it on the bed and smoothed it out. "She wanted us to be there," Lindy said without looking at him. "I'm going to write to her and tell her I wanted to come."

"Why, Lindy?" He sank onto the bed. "Why are you such a big fan of hers all of a sudden? Every time you saw her, you mouthed off to her. I figured you'd be glad she was gone."

"She was nice to me. And she didn't talk to me like I was a kid." She lifted the invitation and placed it carefully on her nightstand. She looked at him. "Are Logan and I always going to live with you?"

Was she worried about Mallory taking them away? "Absolutely. At least until you go to college. You're not going back to your mom's."

"That's not what I mean." She frowned. "I know Mom doesn't want us to live with her. I mean after college. You know, when we're adults. Are we going to live with you then?"

What the hell was going on in her mind? "If you want to," he said cautiously. "You can live here as long as you like. But most kids get their own places when they get a job after college."

"What if I move away from Spruce Lake? To, like, Los Angeles. Or New York."

"Then you'd definitely get your own place," he said. "It would be a pretty long commute every day."

She slid down farther in the bed. "Does that mean you wouldn't love me anymore? If I went away?"

"Of course not." He gathered her into his arms. "You don't stop loving someone just because they go away. You're my little girl. I'll miss you, but I'll always love you, no matter what. No matter where you are."

She leaned away from him. "Would you come to see me?"

"Whenever I could."

She flounced up with a triumphant grin. "Then how come you don't want to see Fiona, just because she went away?"

Damn it. He hadn't expected a trap from his kid. "That's different, Lindy. She's not my daughter."

"But you love her, don't you?"

"It's not the same."

"Why not?" Lindy persisted.

"It's just not, okay?" He stood up. "Go to sleep, Lind. It's late."

As he kissed her good-night, his gaze

dropped to the torn and taped invitation next to her bed. He squeezed his daughter's shoulder and walked out of the room.

TUXEDOED WAITERS SLIPPED through the crowd with trays of Veuve Clicquot and appetizers from the most exclusive caterer in Manhattan. A bow-tied bartender stood behind a small bar at one end of the gallery, dispensing drinks. The pieces Fiona had selected for the show were carefully displayed in glass cases, on artfully draped black velvet.

Jules Clybourne had gone all out for her show. And she'd lived up to her reputation as one of the most influential gallery owners in Manhattan by drawing huge crowds.

Fiona's feet ached in her Jimmy Choo stilettos, and the skirt of her Armani suit made it impossible to walk with her normal long strides. But they were her armor. Her New York persona. Famous jewelry designer. Successful businesswoman. A force in the art world.

She touched the pendant she wore around her neck, the one Lindy had helped her make. She'd hoped Lindy would be there to see it. But Jackson and his kids hadn't shown up.

Zoe and Gideon were there. So were Bree

and Parker and Charlie. All her friends from the city had come, too.

Her new designs were proving to be an unqualified success. Almost all of the pieces were already sold, and as the evening wore on, several guests had gotten into polite bidding wars over the remaining pieces.

Charlie sidled up to her. "Aunt Fee, I just found out what escargot is. Did you know they're snails? I almost ate one. That's totally gross."

"They're just a delivery system for garlic and butter," she said with a laugh. "They're very good. You should try one."

Her nephew shuddered. "No way."

She wondered what Logan and Lindy would have thought of the snails. She knew what Jackson would have said. He'd have asked how they went with beer.

"It's really crowded," Charlie said. He studied the sea of fancy clothes and jewelry. "There's too many people to see them all."

"Tell me about it," she said. "It's my job to walk around and talk to each of them."

"So you'll see everyone who's here tonight?"

"Every one of them." No matter how much her feet hurt afterward.

"Cool," he said.

As Charlie wandered off to find food more appealing than escargot, a woman in a Versace gown came over and grasped her hands. "Fiona, what a marvelous show. Your new line is simply fabulous. I adore it."

"Thank you," Fiona answered, trying to place the woman. "I'm glad you're enjoying it."

"I normally don't buy anything from the shows I cover," the woman confided. "But I broke my rule this time. I simply had to have the gold and lapis earrings."

Angela James. The art critic from one of the major New York papers. "Wow, Angela. Thank you. I don't know what to say."

"Say you're going to be continuing in the same vein and expanding your new line of FeeMac jewelry."

"I am." Fiona relaxed. This was her milieu. She knew how to do this, how to schmooze the critics and the buyers. "Let me tell you what I have planned."

Two hours later, the crowd had thinned. Fiona was making one last round of the gallery to make sure she'd spoken to everyone there, when a woman wearing a huge diamond pendant and earrings to match strolled up to her. "You're Fiona McInnes, aren't you?"

"Yes, I am. Welcome to my show."

"I love your jewelry, and there's nothing left to buy," she said. "I'm devastated."

"Jules is going to be selling my new line. We'll have more available in a couple of weeks. Or I can give you the names of boutiques that will be carrying some of the pieces."

"I don't want to wait that long. I want to be able to say I bought my piece at your show. People will be talking about it for months."

"I'm sorry," Fiona said.

"What about that pendant you're wearing?" Fiona stepped back. "Can I buy that?"

"This piece isn't for sale," Fiona said, her hand hovering protectively over the sunburst. "I'm sorry."

"Oh well, that's disappointing. I thought maybe you'd be willing to part with it—it must be special to you."

"Some things don't have price tags. And this necklace is one of them." Fiona smiled. "Copies will be available in a few weeks. But the original isn't for sale."

"Thanks, but I'm not interested in a copy. I'll just have to wait for my FeeMac original."

"Talk to Jules," Fiona said, steering her toward the gallery owner. "She'll be happy to help you."

The show seemed to drag on forever. Every time the door opened, Fiona looked over, hoping to see Jackson walk in with the kids. Every time it shut behind a stranger, her heart ached a little more.

Finally, after everyone but her family had left, Fiona allowed herself to sink into one of the chairs along the wall and kick off her shoes. Zoe dropped into the chair next to her.

"Pretty damn impressive, Fee."

Fiona shrugged. "Jules does a great job."

Her sister gave her a sidelong look. "I'd say it was more than Jules throwing a good party. I've always known how talented you are. Now I can see that a lot of other people think so, too."

"You're going to make me blush, Zo," Fiona said, rotating her sore feet. "It turned out okay."

"Okay? Is that all you can say?"

Jackson hadn't shown up. "It's been a busy few weeks, you know? The show itself is almost anticlimactic."

Zoe leaned toward her. "Did you hear from Jackson?"

"No." Fiona stood up, cringing as she put weight on the balls of her feet. "I've got to help Jules shut down. Do you guys want to get something to eat after I'm done?"

"Sure, you can show us the big city," Zoe said. "We'll go somewhere and celebrate."

"Thanks, Zo." Fiona hugged her. "I wouldn't have been able to do it without the money you and Bree lent me."

"I'm glad we had it. And now that Jamie has found Barb in Florida, you can pay us back when you get restitution. Bree and I are both getting sick of hearing how grateful you are." She hooked her arm through Fiona's. "We'd rather hear when you're coming for a visit."

"Soon, Zo. As soon as I can get away." As soon as she thought she could handle being back in Spruce Lake.

Jules was thrilled with the success of the show, and she chattered away about how it would be one of the year's highlights. Fiona nodded and answered when it was necessary, but as she packed bracelets and earrings and pendants in padded mailing boxes, she wondered why she wasn't happier.

She'd worked a long time for this success. This was what she wanted, wasn't it? After tonight, FeeMac would be acknowledged as a cutting edge, innovative line. Jules had made a lot of money for her. Several boutique owners had approached her tonight. Her career was back on track.

It was what she'd wanted.

She touched the pendant around her neck.

It wasn't enough.

"Can you close up?" she asked Jules. "I'd like to go out with my family."

"Of course," the other woman said, smiling. "You were wonderful tonight."

"Thanks," Fiona said. "I'll call you, okay?"

Without waiting for an answer, she walked over to Bree and Zoe. "Let's go. I need to talk to you."

CHAPTER TWENTY-ONE

"Come on, Annabelle. Time for a walk."

The dog clearly understood the word *walk*, because she ran in circles barking, then dashed for the door. Smiling, Fiona attached her leash, then left her apartment and pressed the button for the elevator.

"We're having breakfast," Fiona explained to the dog. "At your favorite restaurant." The waitstaff at the little café with outdoor seating spoiled Annabelle shamelessly.

Annabelle wagged her tail as if she understood every word. "I knew you'd be excited."

The sun heated the sidewalk as she stepped out of her building, and Fiona slid on her sunglasses. Annabelle trotted beside her as she headed for the restaurant, two blocks away.

"There she is!" someone behind her shouted. "Fiona! Wait!"

She turned around to see Lindy and her

brother running toward her, and her heart began to pound. "Hey, you guys. What are you doing here?"

"We were supposed to be here last night to go to your show," Logan said.

"But there was a storm in Green Bay." Lindy elbowed her brother out of the way and scooped up Annabelle. The dog wriggled in her arms and licked her face. "Our flight was canceled. We got to sleep in the airport. It was awesome."

Fiona looked past them. Jackson was walking toward her, dressed in rumpled slacks and a wrinkled dress shirt. He shoved his hands into his pockets.

"Hello, Fee," he said when he reached them.

"Jackson." She caught her breath. "What are you doing here?"

"Coming to see you." He put a hand on his kids' shoulders. "We had quite the adventure."

"I wanted to see the show," Lindy said. "Did you sell our necklace? Did you get a lot of money for it?"

"No, I didn't sell it," she said, acutely aware of Jackson's gaze. "It was too special to sell."

Lindy's face fell. "I thought lots of people would want to buy it."

"They did," Fiona assured her. "One woman

tried to pull it off my neck. I had to sic Charlie on her."

"You did not." Lindy watched her skeptically. "Really?"

"I did wear it and lots of people wanted to buy it. It was a big hit. We'll…I'll be making more of them."

"Can I—?"

Jackson squeezed Lindy's shoulder. "Can I get a word in here?"

He stood too close, and Fiona was sure he could hear her heart thundering in her chest. She swallowed. Even though he'd apparently slept in the clothes he was wearing, he still looked good enough to make her mouth water.

"I need to talk to you, Fee," he said.

"Okay." She looked at Logan and Lindy, who were paying close attention. "I was just going to meet Zoe and Bree and the rest of the family for breakfast. You, uh, want to come along?"

"No, thanks." He cleared his throat. "I'm not their favorite person right now. Is there somewhere around here we could wait?"

"My apartment." As she led them back toward her building, she stopped abruptly. "How did you know where I lived?"

"*I* found out," Lindy said proudly.

"How did you do that?" Fiona asked. Only her close friends knew her address.

"Charlie told us," Lindy said. "Logan called him this morning. But it was my idea."

"That was pretty sneaky."

"I know," Lindy said happily.

"Charlie told me you ate snails," Logan said, making a face. "I wish I'd seen that."

The two kids waited expectantly. Were she and Jackson supposed to talk in front of them? "Jackson, why don't you go up to my apartment?" she said. "Logan and Lindy can have breakfast with my sisters and Charlie, and we can talk."

She dug the key out of her purse and handed it to him. "Four A," she said. She took out a piece of paper and scribbled a note. "Give this to the doorman."

Twenty minutes later, she stood in the elevator as it slowly rose, gripping the strap of her purse. Her skin felt too tight. Jackson had tried to come to her show. He wouldn't have come all this way just to blow her off again.

The apartment door was unlocked, and she took a deep breath, then walked in. Jackson turned away from her bookcase as she closed and locked the door.

"Jackson. I'm back." What did he think of

her apartment, with the wild colors and eclectic furniture?

It didn't matter, she told herself impatiently. She stood with her back to the door, wishing she was still wearing her Jimmy Choos and Armani suit from last night. Her armor. She set her purse on the floor and kicked off her flats. The pedicure she'd gotten with Lindy had started to chip. "Would you like something to drink? A cup of coffee?"

"I'd love a cup of coffee."

She didn't look at him as she made him an espresso, but her nerves jumped whenever he moved. He filled her small kitchen, but didn't seem to notice he was making her feel trapped. Surrounded.

When she finally handed him the tiny cup, he stared at it for a moment. "Pretty fancy coffee."

"I figured if you slept at the airport, you'd need a big hit of caffeine."

He sipped it and nodded. "Yeah. Thanks."

She brushed past him and into the living area of her loft. "What are you doing here, Jackson?"

"As the kids said, we tried to come to your show but—"

"I mean, why did you come today? The show's over."

He set the coffee on her counter. "The show wasn't the only reason I wanted to come to New York."

"No?"

"I wanted to see you." He walked toward her, and her heart thudded against her chest. "I have some things I need to say to you."

"I'm all ears." She faced him from the other side of the couch and dug her fingers into the Ultrasuede to brace herself.

He tilted his head and smiled. "You always were a tough nut to crack," he said. "Okay, here's the short version. We can get into the details later. I was an idiot and a fool to let you walk away. I've come to beg you for another chance."

She was gripping the couch so hard, she was going to leave marks. "I don't want you to beg, Jackson."

"How about groveling? I can do that, too, if that's what it takes."

"I just want to know why you changed your mind."

She watched him step around the couch, felt her heart speed up. When he was close enough for her to touch, close enough to smell the faint scent of the aftershave he'd used yesterday and the coffee on his breath, he stopped.

"I love you, Fee. Always have, always will. I don't know how we're going to work this out, but we will. I'm doing what I should have done twelve years ago and coming after you. And I'm warning you, I'm stubborn. I'm not going to give up."

Suddenly she felt warm right down to her toes. She'd been so cold since she returned to New York. "I need to show you something."

She slipped past him to open her desk drawer, pulled out a piece of paper and handed it to him.

He scanned it, then looked up. "This is a ticket to Green Bay. For tomorrow."

"I was coming back. I was going to camp out on your front porch until you changed your mind."

He finally touched her. Cupping her face in his hands, he said, "I'm so sorry. I'd rather cut off my hand than hurt you. And I said the things I knew would hurt you the most."

"I know. And I understand why you did it. I left you once before. How could you know I wouldn't do it again?"

She wrapped her arms around his neck and

buried her face in his shirt, inhaling his scent. She would never get enough of it. She'd taken the pillowcase from the bed where they'd made love and slept with it for the past three weeks, because it still smelled like him.

"I won't leave you, Jackson. I won't run away. I got what I wanted. I got fame and success and recognition. But it didn't mean anything without you." She grasped his shirt in her fists. "Last night, all those people were telling me how great I was and how much they loved my jewelry, and I didn't care. All I cared about was that you weren't there to share it with me. All I wanted last night was to see you walk through the door of the gallery. After it was over, I came home and bought my ticket.

"I love you, Jackson. I never stopped loving you."

He pulled her close and kissed her until her knees weakened. Until she couldn't think of anything but him.

"Will you marry me, Fee?" he asked, nipping at her ear. "Take on all my baggage— my kids, my job, both of our careers?" He kissed her again. "And I'm warning you, I'm not letting you go until I get the answer I want."

"Hmm," she murmured, wriggling closer. "Maybe I'll think about it for a while."

"Take your time," he said.

Sunlight poured through the windows of her loft, bathing them in golden light. She tightened her arms around his neck and poured herself into the kiss.

"Do you have an answer for me?" he said against her mouth.

She nibbled his lower lip, one leg around his. "I'm not finished thinking."

"I guess I'm going to have to take drastic measures," he said, then swept her into his arms.

She was draped across his chest, her heart racing, her muscles limp. Jackson's heart thundered beneath her ear.

He shifted so he could see her face. "If we have to have a commuter marriage, we'll make it work. I've been trying to hire another vet for a while. Once I do, the kids and I can come to New York on weekends."

"And I'll come to Spruce Lake whenever I can." She took his hand. "It won't be like this forever. Once things settle down, once I get my business reestablished with the new line, I can do a lot of it from Spruce Lake. I'll still have to come to New York, but Spruce Lake will be home."

"I know how you felt about that town. It's not going to be a problem to live there?"

"My father was a horrible man and he made our lives hell. But I'm an adult now. At some point, you have to let the past go. You have to take responsibility for your own actions and stop blaming your parents."

"Have you done that?" he asked.

"It took a while, but Zoe, Bree and I finally figured it out. Our father was a narcissistic jerk, but we're not going to let him control us anymore."

"So you're going to be absentminded and absorbed in your work, and I'm going to tease you about it. Does that sound about right?" he asked.

She snuggled into him. "That sounds perfect."

"Logan and Lindy will roll their eyes a lot. Can you deal with that?"

Shifting so she could see his face, she said, "Is this going to be a problem for Lindy? Or Logan?"

"Lindy's the one who dug your invitation out of the trash after I threw it away. And Logan likes you just fine." He grinned. "Especially since visiting you got him out of school for a couple of days. And now he'll be able to brag to his friends that his stepmother eats snails."

He kissed her again. "Although, in the interest of truth in advertising, I have to say, they can be a handful. Lindy especially."

"I was a handful, too," Fiona said. "So Lindy and I will get along just fine." She glanced at the clock. "And we should probably call Bree and Zoe. I told them I needed to talk to you. I'm going to be hearing about our three-hour conversation for a long time."

A half hour later, she and Jackson met everyone in Central Park. As they walked toward their families, hands entwined, Bree and Zoe watched them carefully.

She let go of Jackson, who pulled his kids to the side, and embraced her sisters. "Thank you for watching them," she said. "We're good."

"Yeah, we figured," Bree said. "You can do a lot of talking in three hours."

Fiona smiled. "We did."

"So when's the wedding?" Zoe asked.

"We've already waited years. We'd like to have it at Dad's old house, after the remodeling is finished. A wedding should get rid of any ghosts that are left."

"That sounds perfect," Zoe said.

"Yes, Fee," Bree added. "Perfect."

The three of them clung together. "The McInnes family is back," Fiona said. For what seemed like the hundredth time, she put her hand on Zoe's stomach. "Not only better, but bigger, too."

Bree brushed a tear away. "Go to them," she said nudging her toward Jackson. "We've fixed our family. It's time for you to make a new one."

As she walked over to Jackson, he took her hand, then put his arm around her shoulder. "We're getting married," he said to Logan and Lindy.

"That's cool," Logan said. He held out his clenched hand, and Fiona bumped fists with him.

"Thanks, Logan."

"Lindy?" Jackson said.

"Duh. Whose idea do you think it was to come to New York? So I guess this means you're going to be messing up our house with all your jewelry stuff."

"I'll try to keep my mess under control. But I'll expect you to help me make some of those messes. I figure you probably have a few more design ideas."

"Yeah." Lindy's eyes lit up, and she cleared her throat. "I got a notebook. It's just like yours."

Fiona reached out and hugged both of the kids. "I can't wait to see your designs," she whispered to Lindy.

Lindy clung to her for a moment, then backed up. "Annabelle will want to sleep with me."

"Is that right?" Jackson said. "You already discussed this with Annabelle?"

Lindy rolled her eyes. "You're so lame."

"I'm hungry. What are we going to have for lunch?" Logan asked.

Was it that easy to go from "we're getting married" to "what's for lunch?" Fiona's throat swelled. "They have this great pizza in New York. Want to try it?"

"I want pepperoni," Lindy said.

"We always get pepperoni," Logan said. "It's my turn to get sausage."

"Maybe we could hold off on the bickering for a few days so we don't scare Fiona away?" Jackson suggested.

"You're not going to scare her off," Lindy said. "I already tried that. It didn't work."

Three months later

THE SIDEWALK OUTSIDE the house was covered with bird seed, there were only a few pieces left of the wedding cake and wrapped presents were piled in the living room. Everyone but her family was gone.

They'd ended up around the long table in the new kitchen, like they usually did when they got together. Fiona entwined her fingers with Jackson's.

"What a wonderful wedding," she said. "Thanks, Zoe. Bree."

"You're welcome." Zoe smiled and put her hand over her baby bump. "The kids liked it, too, based on how much they've been kicking."

"That was all the wedding cake you ate," Bree said. "That'll keep them going for a while."

Charlie, Lindy and Logan wandered over to the island in the center of the kitchen to pick at the cake. Gideon rubbed Zoe's back, and Parker lounged next to Bree, his arm across her shoulders.

Fiona looked at the granite countertops, the stainless-steel appliances, the hardwood covering the whole first floor of the house. The office had been eliminated to make the living room larger. "He's gone," she said quietly. "We did it. This is our house now. We made ourselves a family again."

And they each had their own family, as well. She leaned against Jackson. "You're getting more than you bargained for," she said. "Nieces and nephews, sisters and brothers."

"I'm getting exactly what I want," he said. "How about you? How does it feel to have an instant family? Two almost-teenagers?"

"It feels great." Her heart swelled as she looked around the room at her family. "Exactly want I want."

She kissed Jackson. "It feels like home."

* * * * *

*Celebrate 60 years of pure
reading pleasure with Harlequin®!*

*Step back in time and enjoy a
sneak preview of an exciting anthology
from Harlequin® Historical with*
THE DIAMONDS OF WELBOURNE MANOR

This compelling anthology features three stories about the outrageous Fitz-manning sisters. Meet Annalise, who is never at a loss for words… But that can change with an unexpected encounter in the forest.

*Available May 2009
from Harlequin® Historical.*

"I'm the illegitimate daughter of notoriously scandalous parents, Mr. Milford. Candidates for my hand are unlikely to be lining up at the gates."

"Don't be so quick to discount your charms, my dear. Or the charm of your substantial dowry. Or even your brothers' influence. There are as many reasons to marry as there are marriages."

Annalise snorted. "Oh, yes. Perhaps I shall marry for dynastic reasons, or perhaps for property or influence. After all, a loveless, practical marriage worked out so well for my mother."

"Well, you've routed me on that one. I can think of no suitable rejoinder." Ned rose to his feet and extended his hand. "And since that is the case, let me be the first to wish you a long and happy spinsterhood."

Her mouth gaped open. And then she laughed.

And he froze.

This was the first time, Ned realized. The first time he'd seen her eyes light up and her mouth curl. The first time he'd witnessed her features melded together in glorious accord to produce exquisite beauty.

Unbelievable what a change came over her face. Unheard of what effect her throaty, rasping laughter had on his body. It pounded a beat upon his ear, quickly taken up by his pulse. It echoed through him, finally residing in his stirring nether regions.

So easily she did it, awakened these sensations within him—without any apparent effort at all. And she had called him potentially dangerous? Clearly the intelligent thing for him to do would be to steer clear, to leave her to the tender ministrations of Lord Peter Blackthorne.

"You were right." She smiled up at him as she took his hand and climbed to her feet. "I do feel better."

Ah, well. When had he ever chosen the intelligent path?

He did not relinquish her hand. He used it to pull her in, close enough that he could feel the warmth of her. "At the risk of repeating Lord Peter's mistake and anticipating too much—may I ask if you'll be my partner in battledore tomorrow?"

Her smiled dimmed. Her breath came a little faster. His own had gone shallow, as if he'd just run a race—and lost. He ran his gaze over the appealing lift of her brow and the curious angle of her chin. His index finger twitched.

"I should like that," she said.

His finger trembled again and he lifted it, traced the pink and tender shell of her ear, the unique sweep of her jaw. Her pulse leaped beneath her skin, triggering his own. Slowly he tilted her chin up, waiting for her to object, to step back, to slap his hand away.

She did none of those eminently sensible things. Which left him free to do the entirely impractical thing.

Baby soft, the skin of her lips. Her whole body trembled when he touched her there.

He leaned in. Her eyes closed, even as she stood straight against him, strung as tight as a bow. He pressed his mouth to hers. It was a soft kiss, sweet and chaste. And yet he was hot and hard and as ready as he'd ever been in his life.

She drew back a little. Sighed. Their breath mingled a moment before she slowly backed away.

"Oh," she breathed. Her dark eyes were full of wonder and something that looked like fear. He took a step toward her, but she only shook her head. His outstretched hand fell to his side as she turned to disappear into the wood. This was the first time, Ned realized. The first time, since he'd come to the house party at Welbourne Manor, that he'd seen her eyes light up.

* * * * *

*Follow Ned and Annalise's story
in May 2009 in
THE DIAMONDS OF WELBOURNE MANOR
Available May 2009
from Harlequin® Historical*

*Available in the series romance section,
or in the historical romance section,
wherever books are sold.*

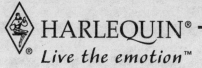

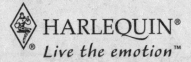

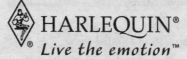

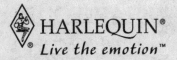

HARLEQUIN® *Presents*

The world's bestselling romance series...
The series that brings you your favorite authors,
month after month:

Helen Bianchin...Emma Darcy
Lynne Graham...Penny Jordan
Miranda Lee...Sandra Marton
Anne Mather...Carole Mortimer
Melanie Milburne...Michelle Reid

and many more talented authors!

Wealthy, powerful, gorgeous men...
Women who have feelings just like your own...
The stories you love, set in exotic, glamorous locations...

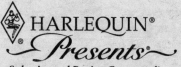

HARLEQUIN® *Presents*

Seduction and Passion Guaranteed!

x

x

x

HPDIR08

www.eHarlequin.com

Harlequin® Historical
Historical Romantic Adventure!

Imagine a time of chivalrous knights and unconventional ladies, roguish rakes and impetuous heiresses, rugged cowboys and spirited frontierswomen—these rich and vivid tales will capture your imagination!

Harlequin Historical... they're too good to miss!

HHDIR06

♥ *Silhouette*®